JFICTION
Feig
Feig, Paul.

**IgnatiusMacfarland: frequency
freak out!**

Ignatius MacFarland:
Frequency Freak-Out!

by Paul Feig

LITTLE, BROWN AND COMPANY
New York   Boston

Little, Brown and Company

Hachette Book Group
237 Park Avenue, New York, NY 10017
Visit our website at www.lb-kids.com

First Edition: July 2010

Little, Brown and Company is a division of Hachette Book Group, Inc.
The Little, Brown name and logo are trademarks of
Hachette Book Group, Inc.

The characters and events portrayed in this book are fictitious.
Any similarity to real persons, living or dead, is coincidental
and not intended by the author.

Library of Congress Cataloging-in-Publication Data

Feig, Paul.
  Ignatius MacFarland, frequency freak-out! / written by Paul Feig ;
illustrated by Shane Hillman. —1st ed.
    p. cm.
  Summary: Twelve-year-old Iggy and his friend Karen find them-
selves transported to an alternate reality, where the trees that rule
a vast underground city are convinced that Iggy and Karen are in
league with the human that stole their gold.
  ISBN 978-0-316-16667-6
  [1. Trees—Fiction. 2. Science fiction.] I. Hillman, Shane, ill.
II. Title. III. Title: Frequency freak-out.
PZ7.F333465Ih 2010
[Fic]—dc22

                                                        2009027473

10 9 8 7 6 5 4 3 2 1

RRD-C

Printed in the United States of America

This book is NOT dedicated to Frank Gutenkunitz
and all the other jerky kids who for some
stupid reason loved being mean to me in school.

Nor is it dedicated to that way stuck-up
Ashley Warner and her dumb friends
Cheryl, Diane, and Becky, who all laughed
at me in front of everybody when I asked Ashley
to the Christmas dance last year.

I thought about dedicating it to
peanut butter and jelly sandwiches
because I really, really like those,
but that seemed like the kind of thing
some weird kid with no friends would do.

Paul Feig wanted me to dedicate this book
to his wife, Laurie, and say that she is his
"best friend" and "the love of his life"
and all sorts of other mushy, embarrassing stuff.

But there's no way I'd ever do that
in a million, kajillion years.

And so I guess I'll just dedicate it to you,
the very, cool, intelligent, classy,
and kind person who was nice enough to pick up
this book and read about my awesome,
dangerous, and totally true adventures.

Hey, bet you never had a book dedicated to you, huh?

You're welcome.

1

Uh...

We were sitting in mud.

Warm, wet mud that was currently soaking through the seat of my pants. As if our clothes weren't dirty enough already from the last frequency we had just visited—a place with no washing machines, but lots of creatures who were more than happy to try to kill us any time of the day or night.

Karen and I looked around in a daze, realizing we weren't back home like we thought we would be. No, we were in the middle of what I would have to call "nowhere." I call it "nowhere" because it was completely empty.

No mountains. No hills. No trees. No plants. No grass. No buildings. No people. No creatures. No things. *Nothing.* It was just an endless flat world as far as we could see, like some huge broom had come down from the sky and swept everything off the face of the earth. The air was hot and muggy, and the sky was filled with big scary-looking black clouds.

I looked over at Karen, my sixteen-year-old hot-headed, kung fu–fighting friend. She was staring at this new deserted world with the same look she might have if she'd walked into a room expecting it to be filled with people she liked and food she loved but instead it was filled with all the kids from school who hated her and all the food she couldn't stand and it turned out it was a Let's-Beat-up-the-Person-Who-Just-Walked-in-the-Room party.

Karen and I looked back to see if the frequency transporter that had brought us here was still behind us. As soon as we did, the machine glowed bright white and then disappeared with a really low-pitched *THUMP* that made my ears pop.

"Oh, man…" was about all I could say. Because

without that transporter, it sure seemed like we were trapped in another frequency.

Again.

See, in case you didn't know or don't remember, Karen and I had just escaped from a different frequency. We had both ended up in *that* frequency because of explosions we had been in back home that had knocked us into the frequency next to ours. Oh, and in case you're really behind on what the whole "frequency" thing means, I'm talking about different realities that exist in the same physical space.

You know, sort of like how a radio has a bunch of different stations inside it that you can select by changing the number on the dial? Or how your computer has tons of different websites inside it that show up if you type in the right address? The stations and websites all come out of the same radio and computer, but each thing that comes out is different. And it's the same thing with frequencies.

The frequency we had just left was filled with lots of weird animal-like creatures who had been ruled by this former English teacher from my school, a guy named Chester Arthur who had also ended up in that same frequency because of an explosion. Mr. Arthur had gone kind of nuts and turned into a dictator who tried to make the creatures do everything he wanted them to do. But then they all ended up rebelling against him and chasing him and this other guy named Herbert Golonski, who was trying to steal their gold, out of their frequency. And when Karen and I got into Mr. Arthur and Herbert Golonski's frequency-jumping machine to follow them back to what we assumed was going to be our home frequency, we ended up here....

Sitting in mud, in a deserted frequency that definitely wasn't our home, with no sign of Mr. Arthur or Herbert Golonski.

...*rrrrrrrrrrrrr RRRRR UMMM - MMBBBBLLLLLLLLLLLLe*...

Distant thunder rolled over our heads like a big bowling ball going down an alley in the clouds. We then heard what sounded like an audience applauding. But it wasn't an audience. It was a major wall of rain heading across the empty landscape right toward us.

"Oh, no..." was all Karen could get out before the wall of rain hit us and swallowed us up, immediately drenching us. Actually, I think she said "oh, *bleep*," but like I said when I told you my last adventure, I don't think the super important things I've done as a Frequenaut should be filled with profanity. So I'll just go with "oh, no" and leave it at that.

The rain was hot and came down hard in huge painful drops. We jumped up to run for cover but quickly realized that there was nowhere to run *to*. There was no possible shelter in any direction for as far as either one of us could see. There was only flat barren ground that was now quickly turning into mud.

As we got soaked by the rain, Karen looked at me and I could see she wanted to shout, "C'mon, let's go!" But since there was no place we *could* go, we both just sort of stood there staring at each other like two stunned zombies. The only good part of all this was we were getting the much-needed hosing down we both required after having run and fought and sweated and crawled through dirt tunnels in the last frequency. But that sure didn't make it feel any better, especially since it's not really too much fun taking a shower with all your clothes on.

"What do we do?" I yelled to her over the sound of the pounding rain, which was as loud as standing in the middle of a cheering crowd at a football game.

Karen glanced around, then stared at me with a look I'd never really seen on her face before—a look of total confusion.

"I have no idea," she said quietly.

And neither did I.

2
Not Singin' in the Rain

My mom used to watch this really old movie all the time that had a scene in it where a guy who had just kissed this girl he liked was walking down the street and it was pouring rain but since he was all happy and in love, he didn't care. He just started singing and dancing and acting like a total nut as he got soaked. My mom used to sing along when she'd watch it and smile and say it looked like it would be so much fun to do what he was doing.

Well, I'm here to tell you that it wasn't.

I mean, maybe if I'd just kissed some pretty girl and was walking back to my house where I knew I could take a hot bath and eat a big bowl of cereal and watch TV as my clothes were tumbling around in the warmth of the laundry room dryer, I would enjoy it. But I was trapped in a world where I couldn't get out of the rain and so I just had to wander around in the mud as I got wetter than I'd ever been in my life, which made me want to find that singing-and-dancing-in-the-rain guy and punch him in the face.

Karen and I were soaked as we walked for what felt like hours. The good thing was that this frequency was pretty hot, because if Karen and I had been stuck in the pouring rain when it was cold, I don't think we would have lasted more than ten minutes without freezing to death. Not that walking around in hot rain was any kind of a treat. It felt like we were in some sort of green-house. I had been in one a few months earlier when our science class took a field trip. It was a pretty inter-esting place, at least until Frank Gutenkunitz found a bag of manure and secretly put a handful of it into my backpack. When we got on the bus to go home, it stunk really bad, and since it was coming from me, everybody thought I had pooped my pants. What a witty guy that

Frank was. Being away from him almost made it worth being stuck in the hot rain.

I was tired from walking for such a long time. And we still didn't know where we were walking to, which meant that we were now walking pretty slowly, like two people trying to find a house we didn't have an address for.

"This is all your fault," Karen suddenly blurted as the rain poured down on our soaking-wet heads.

"*My* fault?" I said in disbelief. "How is it *my* fault?"

"Because you were the one who said you knew how to work the machine! You were the one who moved your fingers over that computer screen. 'Oooh, I'm so smart. I saw how Herbert Golonski did it. Just follow me. I'm a genius.'"

It was bad enough that I was getting blamed for being stuck in this frequency, especially after she had finally been so nice and impressed with me by the time we had left the last frequency. But it was her mocking imitation of me saying those sentences (which I had never even said) that was really insulting, especially since she made me sound like a five-year-old girl.

"Hey," I shot back defensively, now sounding *like* a five-year-old girl. "Don't be mean to me! *You* were the one who said we had to get in the machine in the first place! I was all set to stay there with Foo."

"Oh, shut up about Foo. She didn't really like you anyway."

"What are you talking about? Yes, she did!"

"No, she didn't. She doesn't know *what* she likes. She's like a cat that rubs against your leg. You think it's all in love with you and then you see it do the same thing to the kitchen table."

"Hey, she really liked me," I said. "Besides, what does it matter to you?"

Karen suddenly slowed her walking and, after a few more steps, stopped altogether.

"Are you all right?" I asked, confused.

Karen just stood there, looking out at the horizon in that way you do when you're staring but you're not really looking at anything. And then, all of a sudden, she said, "I don't know what to do."

And then she started crying.

Now *I* had no idea what to do. It's bad enough when people you know start crying because it puts you in a position of just having to stand there as you try to think of something to say to make them feel better. My mom cries at the drop of a hat and usually over really stupid stuff, like missing a turn when she's driving to the mall or when she finds out our mean grandma is coming over for dinner. And I always just have to stand there and hope she'll stop because I have no idea what I'm supposed to say. But when someone like Karen cries—a person so tough you just assume she doesn't even have tear ducts—what do you do? It's like trying to figure out how to cheer up a lion that's been trying to eat you.

"We're never going to get out of here, Iggy."

"You don't know that," I said, trying to be positive, even though she was starting to make me want to cry too.

"Yeah?" she said as she wiped at her eyes. "*How* do

we get out of here? *Where* do we go? Look around, Iggy. There's nothing."

"But there *can't* just be *nothing*," I said, trying to be what my science teacher always called "the devil's advocate."

"Of *course* there can be nothing," she said with a shake of her head. "Do you think every frequency has evolved life? I bet there're *lots* of frequencies without it, just like none of the other planets in our solar system have anything alive on them. Herbert knew that this was one of the dead frequencies and he set the machine so that it would drop us here and now we're trapped and there's no way we'll ever get out of this place. He set us up, Iggy. He got rid of us."

I wanted to keep playing the devil's advocate but, sadly, what Karen was saying sounded like it made a lot of sense. There was no way out of here without a frequency machine and there were no frequency machines anywhere to be seen. *And* there was nothing alive that could help us figure something out. We really were stuck.

And yet...

I suddenly realized I wasn't in the mood to be so helpless, especially since I had just proven myself to be pretty resourceful in the last frequency we were in.

"You know what, Karen?" I said. "I'm gonna get us out of here."

"How?" she asked, sounding surprised that I was suddenly so confident.

"Um...that's the part I haven't figured out yet. But I will. Trust me."

She stared at me strangely, like she was trying to figure out if I was serious. I stared back at her to show her I was. For some reason, her being so depressed and ready to give up made me feel like I really *was* going to figure a way out of there.

"Be my guest," Karen finally said without a hint of sarcasm.

Coming from her, that was the biggest vote of confidence I could ever have gotten.

I just needed to figure out what to do, which was the hard part.

As we both stood there in the rain and looked around, I saw the first positive thing I'd seen since we had gotten here.

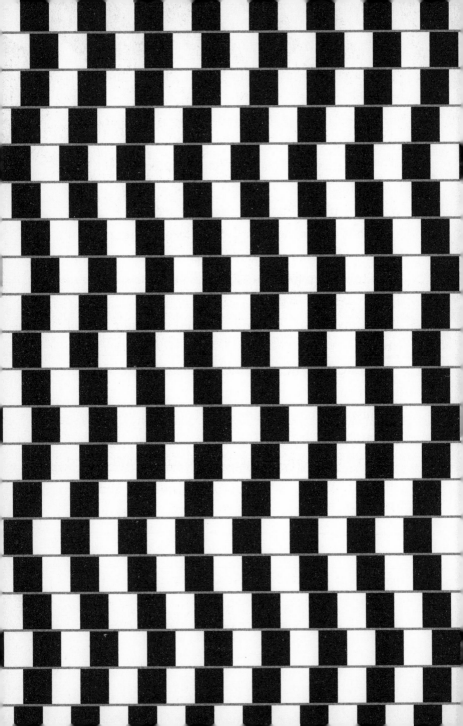

3
We Are Not Alone

It's not often that seeing a weed counts as an exciting event in one's life. But when one is in a place that's devoid of everything except mud and rain, seeing a weed is about as exciting as finding a million dollars.

Well, *almost* as exciting.

Through the driving rain, I saw a small lump about twenty feet ahead of us that looked sort of like a dandelion, only instead of having a yellow flower it had a spiky red one. The rain was pounding down on it pretty hard and from the way it was bent over, it looked like it was in bad shape.

"Karen," I said as I pointed at the weed, "I don't think this frequency is completely dead."

Karen saw the weed and looked surprised. We both ran over and stared down at it. It was bigger than a normal dandelion and had leaves around its base that were long and pointy. The rain was hammering its flower head into the ground and I suddenly felt bad for it, like it was that sad little Christmas tree that Charlie Brown saved on TV.

I kneeled down and picked the flower up out of the mud, being careful not to break its stem. "In *A Charlie Brown Christmas*, Linus wrapped his blanket around the little tree to make it stand up," I said. "Should we wrap something around this?"

"I don't think it'll help. It looks pretty dead."

"I don't think it is," I said as I thought I felt the plant move a little bit.

Karen looked around and then back down at the plant. "That's weird," she said, confused. "Why aren't there any more of them?"

I saw that Karen was right. All around us, there was only rain, mud, and no other plants.

"Maybe all the rest got washed away," I said as I glanced back at Karen. "But at least we know that—"

KA-FOOM!

Mud exploded and the next thing I knew, I was hit hard as something grabbed me around the neck. Karen screamed as I was knocked sideways and suddenly felt like I was being strangled. I turned my head to see what was holding me and was now face to face with the red flower, which was making an angry clicking sound like a sped-up squirrel. Its leaves were clamped around my neck as its spiky petals all pointed at my face. I could see that in the center of its petals it had an eye—just one—that was glaring at me like it wanted to kill me. Two more of its leaves grabbed onto my neck as its roots wrapped around my chest and squeezed so tightly that I couldn't breathe.

Karen jumped and tried to pull the plant off me but the more she tugged on it, the tighter it squeezed.

"Let go of him!" I heard her yelling, as I felt like I was about to pass out. She started pounding hard on its stem and roots, which I knew was supposed to hurt the plant but hurt me way more.

In desperation, Karen grabbed the weed's stem right under its flower head and pulled back on it hard. The weed's angry clicking sound got really fast and high as it dug its leaves deeper into my neck.

"You're…making…it…worse…" I wheezed, feeling like my head was going to pop like an overfilled water balloon.

"Just grab its leaves and help me!" Karen yelled.

As I tried to pry my fingers under its stem, Karen yanked super hard and suddenly the weed let go and leaped at Karen like an attacking tiger. I fell back into the mud and saw Karen grab at her neck as the plant wrapped itself around *her* throat, roots and all. Trying to catch my breath and still woozy from having just been strangled by an attack flower, I jumped up as best I could and ran over to help Karen.

Karen's eyes were bugging out and her face was red. It was clear that the plant had her in an even tighter grip than it'd had on me. It was really trying to kill her.

"Hit…it…Iggy," she gasped. "Do…something!"

I leaped on the weed and tried to do the same thing that Karen had done, first pounding on it as best I could and then trying to grab its leaves. But the stem was wrapped too tightly around her neck, the flower pushing up under her chin as if it wanted to pop her head off like a bottle cap. Karen was trying to speak but all she could make were strangled noises in her throat and

I knew I had to do something quickly. In desperation, I reached in and grabbed onto the weed's red petals like I was about to play a game of "she loves me/she loves me not."

And then I yanked with all my might.

A handful of petals tore off in my hand as the plant squealed and fell off Karen into the mud. Karen dropped to her knees and clutched her throat as she tried to get air back into her lungs while the plant thrashed around on the ground, shrieking and clicking like it was in major pain. A thick green goo was gushing out from where the petals had been pulled off, which sort of made me want to barf.

Then, the weed stopped and gave me the angriest look I'd ever seen in my life. I knew I was in big trouble and started to slowly back away. But the plant made a low, scary clicking noise like an angry dog growling and started to creep toward me on its pointy leaves like the world's most dangerous lobster.

"Uh, Karen," I said quietly as Karen laid there gasping for air. "I've got a big problem here."

SHOOM! The plant leaped straight at me, its pointy leaves sticking out toward my face like daggers. Everything suddenly felt like it was in slow motion as I saw the weed's angry flower face flying at me, now mere inches from my neck. Man, this was not going to be good.

And that was when the last thing in the world I expected to happen happened.

4
Thwack!

In the blink of an eye, the plant was cut in two by a flash of flying metal. The two halves of the plant smacked heavily into my face and chest and then plopped down into the mud, where they twitched for a second and then went limp. I then heard a *shoop-shoop-shoop* sound and saw that the shiny piece of metal that had cut the plant in half was now flying back toward me through the rain. It was some sort of super deadly boomerang.

And before I could move, it spun past my head, just missing me.

I turned to watch it fly away and was shocked to see that there was now a small forest about thirty feet behind me. Before I could spend too much time wondering how I hadn't noticed a bunch of trees just moments before, the tree in the front held out one of its huge limbs and caught the boomerang in mid-air!

The tree was about twenty feet tall and sort of looked like the elm tree in our back yard, except it had big thick leafless branches that looked like huge stiff dreadlocks growing out of its head. And where our elm tree had a tire hanging on it that we used to push each other in, this tree had a belt slung across its trunk with lots of deadly-looking swords and axes and other types of sharp-looking metal blades hanging off it. The tree took the boomerang, wiped the weed's green goo off it, and then clipped the weapon back onto its belt. Then the bottom of its trunk split in two and it began to walk toward me, its big rooted feet slapping onto the ground with every step.

Then all the other trees behind it started to follow. They creaked and groaned loudly as they moved, and the eye at the top of each of their trunks stared at us as they approached.

I looked back at Karen, who was staring back at the tree creatures with a stunned look on her face as she slowly stood up.

"Oh, man…" she said to herself.

"Hey, Karen. Do you think they're friendly?"

"They saved our lives, so just say hello and be nice."

"I'm *always* nice," I said defensively. "*You're* the one I should be telling to be nice."

"Just shut up and say hello, would you?" she said with a roll of her eyes.

I turned back to the trees, which were walking toward us even faster than before, waved my hand, and shouted over the rain, "Hi! Thanks for helping us! We're sure glad to see you. Do you know where there's a frequency transporter we can use?"

The trees walked right up to me and I almost broke my neck looking up at them. They were as tall as two-story buildings, with a few of the ones in the back towering almost forty feet in the air. Their eyes stared down at Karen and me, and I suddenly hoped they weren't the sort of trees that thought it would be fun to stomp one of their big trunk legs down on top of a soaked twelve-and-a-half-year-old kid who had just been strangled by a red dandelion.

I waved again and gave them a big smile, hoping that it would translate as a friendly gesture in whatever language it was that trees spoke.

"My name's Iggy," I said, trying to sound even friendlier. although I think it was just making me sound like I was talking to a baby. "What's yo—"

Before I knew what was happening, the elm tree's limb shot toward me, grabbed me around the waist with all the branches on its big tree hand, and lifted me up into the air so fast I almost got whiplash. At the same time, a super tall willow tree with lots of long, thick branches hanging off the top like hair whipped its arm down and snatched Karen out of the mud as the trees all groaned and creaked in unison.

"Ow! Put me down!" Karen yelled.

I saw Karen trying to struggle out of the willow's grip, but it had her arms pinned tightly to her sides, its thin branch fingers wrapped around her like ropes.

"I don't think they like us," I called out to Karen.

"No duh, Sherlock," she yelled back, although she used a much ruder word than "duh."

The elm tree reached into a pouch on its belt and pulled out a small, flat, ultra high-tech looking silver disc hanging on a strap, which it then hung around my neck. The disc kind of looked like an oversized Olympic medal. That is, until two small lights in the middle of it started blinking and it slowly began to hum, like it was warming up. And then, all of a sudden the elm creaked and the disc made a small beep and we heard a deep male voice say...

"You're under arrest."

Karen and I looked at each other.

"Who said that?" she asked.

"Who do you *think* said it?" we heard the voice say as the elm tree pointed a branch in my face. I realized that the voice was coming out of the disc. The elm tree creaked and the lights on the disc flashed and his voice came out of it again. "Don't play dumb. It's insulting."

"Play dumb?" Karen asked as she tried to squirm out of the willow's branches. "We didn't do anything. Why are we under arrest?"

"Like you don't know," the elm said back.

"Yarg! Stop talking to them," said a deep female voice that also came out of the disc. "You know the rules."

I saw the willow tree holding Karen giving the elm tree a dirty look and creaking loudly.

"I'm the one who taught you the rules, Gree," the elm tree called Yarg said, giving the willow a dirty look back. "So, please don't tell me what to do in front of the prisoners."

"C'mon, you two, no fighting on patrol," said a male voice that was higher than the elm tree's deep rumble.

I looked behind Yarg and saw that it was coming from a tall tough-looking pine tree who was slowly shaking the top of his trunk in disapproval.

"Fine," Gree said impatiently as she whipped her long thin branches over her shoulder the same way Cheryl Biggs used to toss her hair back whenever Mr. Andriasco would yell at her to stop putting on makeup in class.

"Can we just get out of the rain, please?"

"Fine," said Yarg, just as impatiently.

"Actually, if that scout was this close to us," the pine tree said, pointing a branch covered in spikes at the chopped-in-half weed lying on the ground, "we should inspect all our territory up to the border."

Yarg looked at the pine tree and said, "Fiss, our intelligence report shows that—"

"Before you give away all our top-secret data to the prisoners," Gree said in the same sarcastic tone Karen always used with me when she thought I was about to do something stupid, "switch the translator to—"

"*One way*, I know! Get off my trunk!"

I didn't know if trees got married or not but I have to say, Yarg and Gree sure sounded a lot like my mom and dad whenever they got lost trying to drive somewhere.

"If you were in such a bad mood, you shouldn't have come on patrol," Yarg continued as he reached out one of his branch fingers and gave the disc around my neck a couple of taps. "And, you know, it doesn't even really matter if they—"

Yarg's voice cut out and all we could hear was him continuing to creak and groan at Gree in tree language.

"Wait, don't turn it off!" Karen yelled. "Iggy, turn it back on."

"I can't get my hands out," I said as I tried to pull my arms free from Yarg's branch fingers that were wrapped around my entire body.

As Karen and I spoke, we heard creaks and groans come out of the disc as it let the trees understand everything Karen and I said while not translating a word that they were saying. It was *so* not fair.

"Oh, great," said Karen with a shake of her head. "Just freakin' great."

The trees all turned and started walking back where they had come from. And I realized that wherever they were going, we were going with them, whether we wanted to or not.

5
C'mon and Take a Tree Ride

Sometimes I get jealous of babies.

I mean, it's not that I want to be drinking out of a bottle or getting to pee and poo in my pants without anybody getting mad at me. (Although there are times that wouldn't be bad, like when you drink too much soda in a movie theater and can't go to the bathroom because you don't want to miss anything.) I just mean that since I'm basically sort of a lazy person, whenever I see babies getting pushed around in strollers or sitting in harnesses hanging around their mothers' necks, I always wish somebody would do all the work for me when it comes to getting around in life.

However, now that I was truly being carried somewhere by something way bigger than me, I was quickly learning that leaving your transportation up to someone else is not always such a fun thing.

For one, the tree was holding me so tightly with its hard wooden branches that I thought my ribs were going to break. And I was getting all kinds of junk in my eyes because its rough and dusty leaves were pushed right into my face. *And* I was getting shaken and jostled so much as they walked that if I were a can of root beer, I would have exploded already.

I looked over to see Karen and noticed that she was having an even worse ride than I was. Gree the lady willow tree walked like she thought she was a supermodel. She swung her long arms back and forth in huge sweeping half circles which made it look like Karen had been strapped into the world's worst carnival ride.

"Are you okay?" I called over to her. I really had to yell because of the pouring rain and all the super loud creaking and groaning of the trees as they walked. "Karen? Can you hear me?"

"I think…I'm going…to throw…up," she yelled back as she swung.

"Can you see where they're taking us?"

"I can't…see anything. Can you?"

I strained my neck around as much as I could. Ahead of us was just an endless world of dark wet mud and rain.

"It doesn't look like we're going anywhere," I called over as the tree dug its branches even tighter into my sides to get me to stop talking. "And if they're taking us *somewhere*, it's so far away that I don't think my ribs can survive the trip."

"*Your* ribs can't survive?! At least you're not getting swung around like somebody's purse!"

"Hey, *you're* the one who wanted something to happen," I said. "Well, congratulations. It's happening."

"Iggy, you are *so* not amusing," she said as she swung past me again.

Just then, the trees stopped walking.

"Why'd they stop?" Karen called to me from behind the willow tree.

"I don't know," I called back. "Maybe one of them has to go to the bathroom."

"Trees don't go to the bathroom," she said, like I was an idiot.

"Hey, trees don't usually walk or throw boomerangs either, so give me a break."

Yarg stamped his foot three times, sending mud flying everywhere and practically shaking the fillings out of my teeth. I looked around at the other trees and saw they were all looking down at the ground in front of us.

And that was when I heard the rumble.

The ground in front of us split in two. At first I thought some kind of earthquake was taking place, since the ground was moving and a deep vibrating sound was rattling my eardrums. But the crack in the mud just kept opening up slowly and steadily. It seemed that whatever was happening was *supposed* to be happening.

The edges of the crack were smooth and straight and the opening was about thirty feet wide. It was a big sliding door! Mud poured into the gap and I saw it spilling through a dark metal grate a few feet down.

"It's the entrance to some underground place," I called out to Karen. "That's why we couldn't see where they came fr—"

Gree suddenly let out a loud high-pitched crack, like she was yelling at Yarg. Yarg creaked back at her like he was mad and suddenly held me up in front of his eye and put a branch over my mouth, which felt like getting hit in the face with a broomstick. He then groaned and gave me an angry look that I interpreted as "shut up."

"Sorry," I said as best I could with a branch smooshing my lips against my teeth.

The door was now wide open. The trees stepped in and started walking down metal stairs. As we went deeper and deeper into the dark hole, the rain and mud continued to pour in, making wet echoey sounds as it fell through the grates and sloshed down some sort of drain below us.

Once we were deep inside the hole, the trees stopped and the door above us slid shut.

BOOM.

We were now standing in pitch blackness. I tried not to freak out. Ever since I was a little kid, I didn't like being in the dark and until the day I blew up my rocket and became a frequenaut I always slept with a nightlight on. It wasn't something I was proud of, since my dad used to give me lots of grief about it. I guess nightlights are the kind of thing that drive dads crazy, just like not finishing your dinner or crying after you get hit by a pitch in Little League.

Fortunately, before I could have a full-fledged panic

attack, there was a big *KA-CHUNK* and an enormous door in front of us started to lower, clinking loudly as it went down. Bright light flooded in and it suddenly felt like a hot sunny day.

I squinted as the door finished lowering into the ground. As my eyes began to adjust, I wasn't sure if what I was seeing was real or not. Because if it was real, it was almost too crazy to believe.

There in front of me was an entire underground city built completely out of metal girders. It was filled with thousands of tree creatures of all shapes and sizes and went down into the ground so deep that I could barely see the bottom. And it was so wide that you could have put an entire airport inside its walls—with runways and everything!

It was laid out like the world's biggest shopping mall, with level after level of floors that looked out onto an enormous open area in the center. There were walkways crisscrossing the city at all angles so that you could walk from one level to another without having to climb up and down stairs. I didn't see any stores or restaurants, and because the entire city was so drab and colorless, it sort of looked like an enormous prison.

All the tree creatures were walking in a really orderly fashion on the different levels, with short bushy trees

walking around on the higher floors, the medium-sized fatter trees on the next level down, and the bigger tall trees on the lower floors. Walking around in the open middle section were huge trees that were as tall as redwoods and sequoias.

Overhead, there were huge, long lights in the ceiling that were so bright you couldn't look at them. I remembered from a nature show my dad made me watch once that most trees need sunlight to live. Well, this place was bright enough to keep a lot of trees alive for a long time, even though the sunlight was fake.

Yarg walked to the railing on the top level and made an eardrum-rattling groan that echoed all over the city. The trees stopped what they were doing and looked up at us. Gree came up next to me, and then she and Yarg held Karen and me out over the deep center area so that all the trees could see us.

Yarg made a bunch of creaking sounds and pointed at Karen and me with his other huge branch. Suddenly, all the trees in the city started making really loud and angry snaps and groans as they pointed up at us and shook their fists. I looked down and saw that the translating disc had flipped up and was now sitting on one of Yarg's fingers right underneath my chin. I quickly bent my face down and tapped the disc a couple of times with my nose. It beeped and a green light flashed.

"—and will be punished to the full extent of the law!" Yarg's voice blasted out of it as he finished whatever sentence he had started a few seconds earlier.

The trees in the city all made noise again and lots of different voices came out of the disc, saying things like, "Finally!" and "It's about time!" and "Cut them in half!"

I looked over at Karen, who looked back at me and shook her head.

"We're in trouble again, aren't we?" I asked, pretty sure of her answer.

"Yep," she said, sounding fed up. "We're in trouble again."

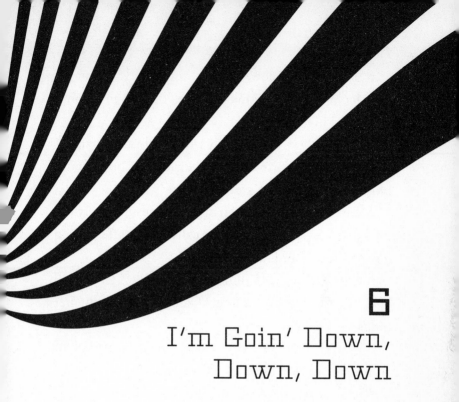

6
I'm Goin' Down, Down, Down

Yarg, Gree, Fiss, and the rest of the tree creatures from patrol paraded us through the entire city, going slowly down the walkways, holding us up so that all the other trees could get a close look at Karen and me. I had never seen a tree with an eye before that day and yet now I was looking at thousands of the angriest tree eyes I could ever imagine. Which wasn't fair at all since I was in 4-H back home and even got a Cub Scout merit badge for planting trees one summer.

"Not so tough now, are you, tough guy?" a maple tree–looking guy with his branches tied up in a pony-tail yelled in my face.

"Oh, you are in *so* much trouble, troublemaker," a skinny creature covered in cherries and bright pink blossoms creaked at Karen.

"You should be ashamed of yourselves," a really old redwood whose bark was practically falling off boomed down at Karen and me.

"WOULD SOMEBODY PLEASE TELL US WHAT WE DID?!" Karen yelled at the top of her lungs.

"YARG!" Gree yelled as she looked at the translator around my neck. "Didn't I tell you to—?"

"I *did* turn it to one-way," he growled at her, angry but trying to be quiet because he seemed embarrassed that she was yelling at him in front of all the other trees. "He must have turned i—"

Click. Yarg touched the disc again and we were once more left with only the sound of creaking trees.

"I'm telling you, the minute they let go of me I'm going to kick some serious tree butt," Karen growled as she struggled uselessly against the tight branches around her.

Our endless walk of shame finally finished when we

got to the bottom level and headed over to a big open area that was roped off with metal chains. A bell rang and a big black door in the floor started to slide open. As it did, Yarg reached over to grab Karen from Gree. I saw that Karen was ready to escape as soon as Gree loosened her grip, but as soon as she unwrapped her branches from around Karen, Yarg spun his around her body to quickly replace Gree's willowy fingers. Once they had made the trade, Gree and the other trees that captured us all gave big creaky bows to Yarg and then walked heavily away.

"Herbert Golonski, you are such a dead man if I ever see you again," Karen said as Yarg started to walk down a huge circular staircase.

We went down deeper and deeper and it got darker and darker, as the door above us slammed shut. I started to wonder if we were going to go down so deep that we'd start to feel the heat of the earth's core. I know you'd have to go pretty far down into the earth to get near anything that hot. But since I had never been further underground than the time Gary and Ivan buried me up to my neck in the sand at the beach and then put Fritos all over my head so that I got attacked by seagulls, I didn't really know how deep you had to go until you got to the fiery center of our planet. But I'll tell you that it was definitely stuffy and really humid and super dark down wherever it was we were going, and again it was hard not to have a panic attack.

We finally got to the bottom of the stairs and walked through a huge archway into what I can only describe as some sort of enormous dungeon. Against the back wall were lots of what appeared to be jail cells, and when I looked closer, I could see trees inside some of them. A huge Christmas tree–looking creature was sitting on the floor in one cell, creaking quietly to itself. In the cell next to that was a smaller maple with crusty bark that was leaning against the bars and tapping its branches absentmindedly as it stared off into space.

Yarg stopped at a smaller jail cell and with one of his many free branches whipped a key off his weapons belt and unlocked the door. And before we knew what was happening, he shoved Karen and me in, grabbed the translator disc from around my neck, pulled his branches out, and slammed the door shut. Karen ran at the door, crashing into it as if she could somehow break it down. *PLANG!* She hit the metal bars so hard that I was sure she broke her shoulder.

"Ow," was all she said as she grabbed her arm and then leaned heavily against the bars, looking completely depressed.

As I watched Yarg walk away and head back up the stairs, I tried to think of something to say to Karen.

But I couldn't.

What was there to say? We were deep underground; we were in jail; and now we couldn't talk to anybody.

In case you didn't notice, we weren't having a very good day.

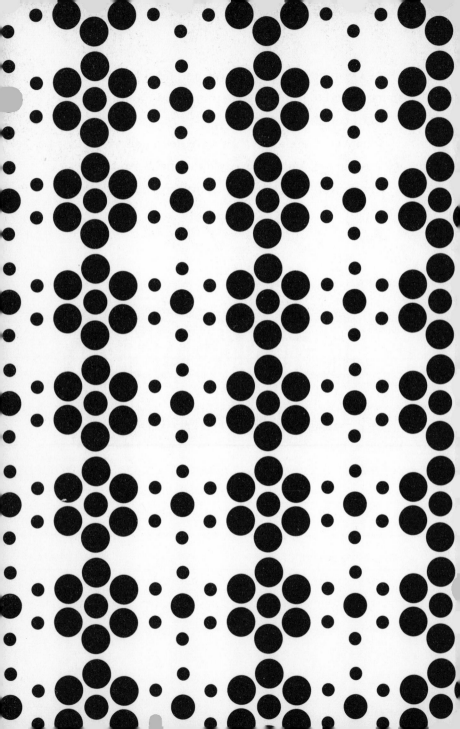

7
Creak

I heard a creak.

So did Karen.

And it came from inside the jail cell.

There was something in the shadows behind us.

"Hello?" I said nervously, feeling like I was about to load my pants.

"Who's there?" said Karen in her tough voice. There was silence for a few seconds, and then we heard what sounded like someone shaking a bag of leaves really fast. "Show yourself!" Karen yelled.

"They don't understand English, remember? Try creaking or something."

Karen ignored me and started to move toward whatever was in the cell with us. She had her hands up in front of her the way kung fu guys do when they're expecting a fight. I'd seen Karen's hands like that before and always felt sorry for whoever was about to get hit with them.

"Be careful," I said, wishing I was anywhere but the cell at that moment.

Then, just as Karen was about to step into the shadows, there was a *whoosh* as a six-foot-tall palm tree flew out of the darkness, grabbed Karen's wrists with two of its fronds (which is what you call the big spiky leaves on a palm tree), and pinned her up against the wall, slamming its long, thin trunk against her legs to keep her from kicking. In the same instant, the palm tree turned its head and stuck another of its fronds straight out at my face, the sharp pointy tip about a millimeter from my nose as if to say, "Don't move."

I raised my hands in the air like someone in a Western who has just been told by a bad guy to "Stick 'em up" and blurted out, rather embarrassingly, "Please don't hurt me!"

Karen struggled to get free of the palm tree but the more she fought, the harder it pushed her against the wall.

"Let me go!" she yelled.

The tree turned its eye back to Karen and tried to stare her down. Karen stared back at it angrily and, even though they weren't saying anything, it was one of the most intense showdowns I'd ever seen. They were giving each other the evil eye so hard that I thought flames were going to come out of their pupils and make each other's heads explode.

And then suddenly, as if some unspoken understanding had occurred between them, the palm tree let Karen go.

Karen stumbled forward but quickly caught herself. I knew her well enough to know she hated any moment that showed she wasn't completely in control and so I pretended I hadn't seen her almost fall flat on her face. She pushed the hair out of her eyes and glared at the palm tree, which slowly walked back into the shadows.

"Are you okay?" I asked her, my heart still pounding from our encounter with the scariest tropical tree ever.

"Of *course* I'm okay," she snapped at me, clearly upset that she'd been overpowered by everything she'd met since we first arrived in this frequency.

"What do we do now?" I asked.

She gave me a fed-up look. "We have a party with lots of cake and ice cream. And then a clown will come and make balloon animals. Got any other questions?"

I wasn't in the mood to fight with her, so I just sat down on the floor and leaned against the wall.

Karen was staring into the shadows after the palm tree. I could tell that she wanted to try to talk to it but before she could even try, the cell door flew open again. Two limbs shot in and wrapped around Karen and me. And the next thing I knew we were being pulled out the door.

Yarg held us up to his eye, gave a sharp snap sound that seemed to say "Don't mess with me," and then carried us off to a huge black door at the far end of the dungeon.

I didn't know what was about to happen but I was pretty certain there wasn't going to be any cake and ice cream in that room.

8
The Oak-Filled Room

It was so bright inside that my eyes hurt.

The place looked like some kind of all-white interrogation room from a police show. I immediately wondered if they were going to do something really bad to us in here, since it seemed like the kind of room where nothing *good* could happen.

We had been transferred from Yarg's branches to the twiggy but strong vines of two squat stumpy bushes that had our arms and legs bound up. They also had vines around our waists that were pulled so tightly we were basically locked into them like two really scratchy, uncomfortable car seats.

SCREEECH!

A chill ran up my spine as Yarg pushed a long metal table up in front of us that made a loud, high-pitched sound as it scraped across the floor. Nails on a chalkboard have always given me the willies and this sounded like a thousand cats all running their claws down a blackboard at the same time.

Yarg was standing at the far end of the table, just staring at us, his eye going from Karen to me and then back to Karen. Karen was breathing hard, clearly getting madder by the minute, and I was just hoping that she wouldn't do or say anything to get these tree people any angrier at us than they already were.

The door opened and three big, impressive-looking oak trees came in and stood next to Yarg. But they didn't look like him. These oaks were perfectly shaped with large leafy tops and big solid branches. Their bark wasn't like Yarg's bark, which was pretty rough and lumpy looking. Instead, these trees had smooth, almost shiny bark that didn't have any spots or scars on it. As soon as they walked up next to Yarg, he stepped aside and gave a grand bow to them. Then these big-shot trees stared at Karen and me for what felt like five minutes.

"I swear to God, if everybody doesn't stop staring at us..." Karen said as she seethed.

Finally, the trees all looked over at Yarg and creaked something at him. Yarg pulled out the translating disc, tapped it, and slid it across the table so that it stopped in the center. The front oak tree leaned forward and creaked. The disc beeped and a very scary voice came out of it.

"Where's our gold?"

And suddenly Karen and I understood everything.

"Oh, man," Karen said as she gave me a look. "Herbert's been here."

"Yes," said the tree, "Herbert *has* been here. And we want our gold returned to us. *Now*. So tell us where it is or we will chop you in half."

"Look," said Karen, sounding like a kid trying not to get in trouble with her parents, "we know who you're talking about. We were just somewhere else with him and he did the same thing to the people there. We actually stopped him from stealing *more* of their gold. So, please don't think that we have anything to do with him."

"You *look* like him," the tree said, as if it had caught Karen in a lie.

"Uch," she said, grossed out. "First of all, please don't say I look like him. Where I'm from that would be a huge insult. And secondly, don't assume that just because we're the same species that Herbert and I think the same way. I hate the guy as much as you do."

Suddenly the front tree slammed its branches down on the table so hard the whole room vibrated.

"We want our GOLD!"

Karen and I jumped back in surprise, hitting our heads against the guard bushes.

"This is ridiculous," Karen said, struggling to stand up. "If you'd tell your guards to untie us it would be a lot easier to tell you what we know about Herbert."

"You can tell us everything you know from exactly where you are," said Yarg, who was now walking forward with a threatening look in his eye. "And I suggest you talk fast."

Karen sighed impatiently as she realized we weren't going to be freed from these bushes anytime soon, then started to talk.

She told the trees all about how Chester Arthur had jumped frequencies and tried to be a dictator in his new world and how Herbert Golonski used this to turn the creatures of that frequency into slaves whom he made dig up tons of gold, which he then transported back to our frequency. She let them know that both Chester and Herbert had tried to capture her from the minute she got there and how Herbert had even wanted to execute her when she exposed his gold-stealing plot.

She told them how I ended up letting the creatures decide to turn against Chester and how they burned down his city and then chased Herbert out of their frequency so fast that he couldn't get all the gold he'd stolen out of there. And then she told them about how we tried to follow him but ended up here. She said that Herbert was a really bad guy and that she had to assume he'd been going to lots of different frequencies to steal gold and apparently this was one he'd already finished with.

The trees all looked at each other, then stared back at Karen and me as if they were trying to figure out if this was just some insane story made up by two people who wanted to avoid being chopped in half.

"What do you mean when you say *frequencies?*" asked one of them.

Karen then explained how each frequency had the same basic materials in it and existed on the same planet but that each frequency had its own set of natural resources, including gold. And because of this, Herbert had apparently decided to steal the gold from every frequency to make himself the world's richest man.

As she was telling them this, I couldn't help but think that it sure was a lot of trouble and work for Herbert Golonski to go through just to become super rich back in our world. But, like my dad used to say, you never know how far people will go just to have a lot of fancy cars and houses.

The trees exchanged looks again, and then one of them pointed at the translating machine. Yarg reached out and tapped it, turning it off. Then the trees huddled together and creaked and groaned and made cracking noises, like they were having some serious discussion.

Karen looked over at me and rolled her eyes. "Like I could make something like this up," she whispered.

The trees finally walked back to the table and turned the translating machine on again. And then, after a long pause, the head tree said...

"We don't believe you."

Karen just sighed and shook her head. "Fine. Then chop us in half."

I looked at her like she was nuts. "Hey, shut up! I don't want to get chopped in half."

"They're not going to believe anything we say, so what's the point of being here anyway? If this is a world where they think we're as bad as Herbert Golonski, then it's a world I have no interest staying in."

She then gave the trees a look that was exactly like the look my mom used to give me when I hadn't taken out the garbage after she asked me to do it about a thousand times. I had to wonder if maybe Karen's attitude would guilt them into realizing that we were actually telling the truth, the same way my mom's look would always guilt me into wheeling all those smelly garbage cans to the street even though it was freezing outside.

"Fine," said the head tree. "Take them back to their cell. We'll chop them in half at dawn."

No, apparently trees weren't that easy to guilt.

9
Yarg

Jail cells are not comfortable.

I mean, I've seen jail cells in movies and on TV and news shows and sometimes if you're a famous guy they have beds and televisions and computers in them and even though you're locked up and can't get out for years, I would look at the cells and think they didn't seem like such terrible places to be. Well, this wasn't one of those cells. There was nothing but wet stone floors and dark metal walls and hard metal bars and

Karen and the world's deadliest palm tree, who was still sitting in the shadows ignoring us.

I was frustrated because our story made so much sense to me that I couldn't figure out how the trees wouldn't believe it. But then I tried to imagine what I would think if some kid showed up in my school and told some wild story about frequencies and creatures and gold. I hated to admit it but I probably would have thought the kid was nuts.

"Do you think they're really going to chop us in half?" I asked Karen quietly, not wanting to disturb the palm tree.

"I doubt it," she said with a sigh. "Without us they have no hope of finding out what happened to their gold, since we're apparently the only humans they've ever seen other than Herbert."

"I can't believe he stole their gold too. How many frequencies do you think he's robbed so far?"

"I don't know," she said in a tone that showed she didn't like me asking questions she couldn't answer. "Who knows how many frequencies there are? However many exist, I have to assume that he's hitting them all. It's actually a pretty good scam if you think about it. If he wasn't hurting so many people in the process, I'd almost be tempted to admire him."

"Really?" I asked, surprised to hear her say that.

After a few seconds, she said, "No, probably not. I hate greedy people."

"So do I," a deep voice said.

We both looked over and saw Yarg standing at the bars, holding the translating machine. He stuck a branch finger through the bars and motioned for us to step forward.

"I think your story has validity," he said quietly as we walked up to the bars. "But I'm the only one. The leaders think you've been sent here by Herbert Golonski to steal other metals from us. They really do plan on chopping you in half tomorrow. I've been trying to convince them to at least wait so that we can fully interrogate you, but they're too nervous after what happened with Herbert."

"What *did* happen?" I asked, since all we knew was that he had taken their gold but had no idea how.

"He befriended us," Yarg said. "He came to our city many rings ago and told us that our enemies were planning a catastrophic attack and that they were going to invade our city and take all our gold."

"And you guys *believed* him?" Karen asked as if *she* couldn't believe it.

"Not at first," said Yarg. "But the more time he spent

with us, the more information he had that seemed compelling. He told us stories about secret weapons they possessed and information they had about our city's security system. Eventually the leaders began to worry that our gold supply truly *was* vulnerable. And that was when Herbert convinced them to let him move all our gold to a safe location."

"Oh my god," said Karen in disbelief. "They *gave* him all the gold?"

"I told them not to do it but he had won them over," Yarg said, beginning to sound angry at the memory of it all. "And so one day they loaded up all our gold and several of our guards escorted Herbert off to a secret location. And we never saw our gold again."

"Did the guards ever come back?" I asked.

"No," he said sadly. "They were found days later. They'd been ambushed. You should have seen them. I never knew our enemy was capable of being that deadly against us."

"So he just rolled your gold right out of here, had somebody kill your guards, and then simply transported the gold back home?" Karen asked, sounding shocked at how easily Herbert's plan had worked.

"Well, that's what I now see might have happened," Yarg said. "The assumption has always been that he was working with our enemy and that he brought our gold directly to them. But hearing what you say about these frequencies and Herbert's ability to move between them, I'm starting to wonder if everything we've believed since we lost our gold is wrong."

"So you believe us now?" Karen asked.

Yarg stared at Karen and me for a second.

"My name is Yarg," he finally said.

"Yeah, we figured that out when your lady friend was yelling at you." Karen chuckled.

"Oh, Gree, yes," he said, sounding more than a bit embarrassed. "My wife."

"I'm Karen and that's Iggy," she said as she gave Yarg a nod.

"Iggy?" said Yarg as his eye looked at me. "That's a strange name."

"Oh, yeah, and *Yarg's* really normal," I said sarcastically before I realized it had come out of my mouth. I didn't mean to be a wise guy, but I'm a bit sensitive about people making fun of my name.

"It's just an odd word," said Yarg apologetically. "You're not hearing it in our language. This is what it sounds like to us."

Yarg tapped off the translating machine and then made a noise that sounded like a huge fart. Then he turned the machine back on.

"See?" he said.

"Oh, great," I said as I put my face in my hands. "Is there a frequency where I'm not a total dork?"

"Yarg, can you get us out of here?" Karen asked.

"Not yet," he said. "I still need to present my thoughts to the leaders and get them to consider it. Then I can bring you to see them again, and you can tell them more."

"I told them everything already," Karen said impatiently. "It's up to them to believe me."

"They were already deceived once by Herbert Golonski," Yarg said, sounding angry. "Be happy I'm getting you a second chance. The only reason you aren't dead already is because of me. For all I know, they're right and you *could* be here setting us up for another theft of our metals."

"We don't *care* about your stupid metals," Karen snapped at him.

Yarg's eye narrowed as he gave Karen a suspicious look. "That's exactly what Herbert Golonski said." He then turned and started to walk away.

Karen looked a bit guilty and pushed her face through the bars.

"Well, can we at least get some food?" she called to him.

Yarg stopped, looked back at her, then walked out of view for a minute. He came back with a bucket and a light, opened the door and slid them in. The bucket was filled with wet dirt. Yarg turned on the light. A thin, bright beam of fake sunlight shined out of it onto the floor. Then he pulled the door shut.

"Is this what Herbert used to eat?" she asked as she wrinkled her nose.

"We assumed so," said Yarg with a shrug of his leaves. "It was what we put in his room every day. He never complained about it."

And with that, Yarg turned and went out the big metal door and up the stairs back to the tree city.

As Karen and I stared at the bucket of dirt in disbelief, suddenly the palm tree walked up between us, picked up the bucket and the light, and headed back into its corner. It stood in the bucket of dirt, adjusted the light so that it shined onto its leaves, and then leaned against the wall to take a nap.

"Hey, that's *our* food," I called over to it, trying to sound tough.

"Iggy," Karen said with a shake of her head. "Let it have the bucket of dirt."

And with that, she sighed, sat down against the wall again, and closed her eyes.

Man, being in jail blows.

10
Attack!

Karen and the palm tree were asleep.

I wasn't.

I tried to sleep but couldn't get comfortable because I was lying on the hard floor and now had to go to the bathroom, which was going to be difficult since there was no toilet in the cell. It's impossible to sleep when your bladder is full because your whole body keeps yelling at your brain to go pee already. And so, after I made sure that both Karen and the palm tree were asleep, I quietly took the bucket of dirt into my corner and relieved myself into it. I figured that the palm tree had used up whatever nutrients were in the dirt and so it was just leftover garbage, like an empty banana peel. But as soon as I was finished, I got hit with a wave of guilt. Did I just pee into the palm tree's lunch box? Maybe when it woke up it'd get back in the bucket to have breakfast and realize what I had done and then beat the crap out of me. I was so paranoid that now there was no way I could go to sleep.

And that's the state I was in when the alarm bells went off.

At first it was a faint ringing coming from the circular stairs. But suddenly the whole jail cell exploded with super-loud bells clanging insanely fast.

"What's going on?!" Karen asked as she automatically struck her kung fu stance.

"I don't know," I yelled over the clanging.

Just then, Yarg came bursting through the stairway door. He ran faster than I would have expected for a tree his size.

"Yarg!" Karen yelled. "What's happening?"

"Enemy attack," he called over as he held up the translating machine.

"Let us out," she said. "We can help you fight."

"No you can't," he said as he got to another door at the far end of the dungeon. "Just stay here. You'll be safe. But keep this in case anybody needs to tell you anything."

He threw the translating disc to me through the bars like a Frisbee.

"Be careful with it," he yelled back as he went through the door. "It's the only one Herbert left us."

Then the door slammed behind him as Karen hit the bars with her fists.

"Ugh!" she yelled. "I am not going to sit in this freakin' cell anymore! We've gotta get out of here!"

"Yarg said we'd be safer down here," I said, hoping that she would just calm down.

Suddenly the palm tree jumped out of the shadows and before we knew what it was doing, it wedged the top thinner half of its trunk through the bars, twisted itself sideways, and *PANG*! The latch on the cell door broke and the door swung open.

"Why didn't it do that before?" Karen gasped, surprised.

"Because it wasn't time yet," said a cool guy voice that came out of the translator. We both looked at the palm tree, who pulled his upper half out of the bars and did a weird, suave one-eyed wink at Karen.

"Nice knowing you," he said. And with that he took off running out of the cell and up the circular stairs.

"Oh, sweet!" Karen said as I saw her eyes fill with excitement. "Iggy, c'mon!"

She took off running after the palm tree and, not wanting to sit there by myself, I hung the translator around my neck and sprinted after her.

We got to the top of the stairs and saw that the entire underground city was scrambling to get ready for a fight. Trees were strapping on weapons belts and armor and grabbing long staffs that had sharp-looking blades on top. The bigger trees were wrapping long metal bands with lots of protruding spikes and sharp edges around their lower trunks and legs. Remembering how unhappy the trees had been to see Karen and me just hours earlier, I realized that we'd better not draw any attention to ourselves with all these metal weapons around.

I grabbed Karen and pulled her behind a big metal pillar.

"This looks really dangerous," I said, trying to talk some sense into her. "Let's at least wait to see what happens."

A loud "*WOO HOO!*" came out of the translating machine.

We both turned and saw the palm tree weaving his way through all the huge redwoods at top speed. When he got to the other side of the open area, he leaped in the air and grabbed onto another support beam with his fronds. He quickly climbed up it, using his bend-able body and thin root feet to scale it like the world's fastest inch worm. Then he flipped from level to level, looking more like Spider-Man than any palm tree I'd ever seen.

"Whoa," Karen said quietly to herself as she watched the palm tree's gymnastic skills.

"It's the traitor!" we heard a deep voice yell through the machine and saw one of the redwoods pointing at the palm tree. "Don't let him escape!"

But there was too much noise for most of the other trees to hear this as the palm tree kept climbing and then disappeared from our view.

Loudspeakers crackled to life and heavy creaking and snapping came echoing out of them.

"Wave one fighters. Wave one fighters. Report to battle lift immediately," said a voice through the translating machine.

Lots of medium-sized trees with big, sturdy trunks and thick, rough branches moved as fast as they could over to a huge door that was lifting open.

As they all headed into what I assumed was the battle lift, Karen looked at me and said, "I'm not staying down here. I've gotta see what's going on."

"You're gonna get us killed," I blurted, starting to panic. "We almost got wiped out by one little weed the last time we were up there. Can you imagine what's going to happen if this enemy of theirs is really launching some kind of full scale attack?"

"Iggy, I don't trust the trees not to kill us any more than I trust whatever's up there. So stay down here if you want to but I'm going to check things out."

I didn't know what to do but since my odds of survival always seemed to be a bit better with Karen nearby, I decided I should be there to offer whatever lame help I could. And so I took a deep breath and ran off after her.

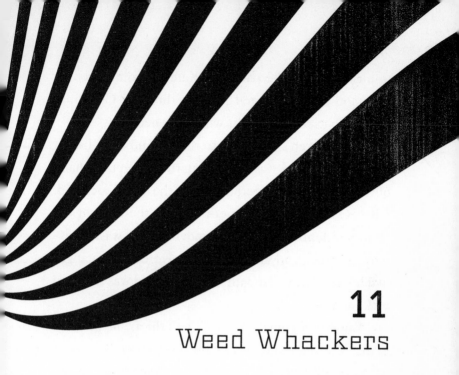

11
Weed Whackers

The underground city was crazy tall because the trees who lived in it were so huge. So after running up two walkways I was completely out of breath. Part of this was because we had to dodge and dart in and out of trees who were swinging around their huge swords and blades and yelling that the "gold stealers" were escaping as they saw us. One big leafy tree that looked like the oak in my grandma's back yard swung a branch right at Karen like she was a baseball and he was trying to hit her out of the park, but Karen hurdled over his limb and then zigzagged through three fat Christmas trees who tried to grab her with their needles.

I used Karen's diversion to run behind their backs. I felt proud that I was actually starting to get the hang of how to dodge dangerous things the way Karen did. That was, until I felt something grab the back of my shirt. Suddenly my feet were moving but *I* wasn't anymore. I turned and saw that a tree covered with oranges had hooked my collar with his branch and was trying to pick me up.

"You're not going anywhere, you thief," he groaned at me as he started to lift me off the ground.

"Karen!" I yelled, but before the last letter of her name crossed my lips, she came flying through the air, grabbed onto the branch that was holding my collar, and used it to swing her legs right into the tree's eye.

POW!

She hit him so hard with her feet that the tree made a crack like a gunshot blast and a ton of oranges exploded off his branches, flying everywhere. The tree let go of my collar and held his eye as Karen fell to the ground, then jumped up and tossed an orange at me.

"Keep it for dinner," she said, as she bolted past and continued up the ramp.

We dodged and darted and ran underneath trees as we sprinted up the endless network of walkways. I could see that the door to the city was open, and the rain was still pouring down outside as the tree army headed up the stairs and out to face whatever battle was about to begin.

When we got to the stairs, Karen ran up behind Gree, who was heading up into the rain, and quickly grabbed a couple of swords off the back of her weapon belt. I saw Karen look at the back of Gree's trunk like she wanted to chop a big wedge right into her willow butt to pay her back for the rough ride earlier. But, fortunately, for once Karen controlled herself.

"Here, in case there's trouble," Karen said as she tossed one of the swords at me and took off up the stairs with the other one. The sword was so long and heavy that it was like having a tether ball pole thrown at me. It hit me across the stomach and knocked me onto my butt.

Before I could grab the sword, Gree turned and saw me on the ground.

"Yarg, you worthless piece of wood," she said to herself as she noticed Karen running up the stairs and into the night. "Why can't you do anything right?"

I jumped to my feet, still clutching the orange, and ran after Karen just as Gree reached out to grab me. I sprinted forward right as her willowy fingers whipped across my back like wet gym towels. I was relieved to find that Gree couldn't run like Yarg, who would have caught me easily. I glanced back and saw her give me a dirty look, then pick up the sword and put it back on her belt.

Great, now I don't have a sword, I thought. It's gonna be a lot of fun defending myself with an orange.

As I got to the top of the stairs, the rain hit me hard in the face. Because of the clouds in the night sky, there was no moonlight. Only the light from the underground city coming up the stairway made it possible to see. I noticed that the trees were getting into some kind of large formation. I scanned around for Karen and saw her crouched down far from the trees, clutching her sword as she tried to peer through the rain.

"Do you see an enemy army?" I asked as I squatted down next to her, hoping that the trees wouldn't notice us in the dark.

"I don't see anything," she said as she strained to see the horizon.

There was a loud *KA-CHUNK*, then a low humming sound. We both turned as the ground in front of the trees started moving. It was another sliding door, this one as big as a football field. As tons of mud poured into the widening hole, I realized that this was the battle lift bringing up the "wave one fighters," whatever that meant. Slowly, I saw the fighters' leafy tops begin to appear and wondered why they hadn't just walked up the stairs like the other trees.

And then I saw why.

The wave one fighter trees were all sitting on top of really deadly-looking vehicles that were made out of dark, scary metal.

The vehicles in the first row were sort of like the most terrifying tractors you've ever seen in your life. On the front of each one was a long metal arm with what looked like a huge lawn mower blade on the end of it. The trees in the second row were sitting on these

huge motorized tricycles that had long cables hanging down from metal arms on each side. And making up the back row were large mechanical spiders with two big scissor-like claws sticking out of the front. Each metal spider had a tree sitting on its back, which made it look like big pieces of broccoli were riding on them.

"Holy moley," I whispered as the battle lift locked into place and the last of the tree army ran up the stairs and got into formation.

Then there was silence. Only the pouring rain made any sound as the thousand-tree army stood and stared out at the empty horizon, waiting for something I couldn't see.

A flash of lightning flickered.

And that was when I saw what the trees were waiting for.

For a split second, my eyes focused on what looked like a tornado that had fallen over on its side and was now rolling straight toward us. It was long and low and seemed to spread across the entire horizon. And then it was gone from sight, as the lightning disappeared and the horizon went dark again.

"What is it?" I whispered to Karen as my eyes strained to see more.

"I don't know," she whispered back as she glanced

at the mechanical spiders. "But judging by those machines the trees are riding on, I don't think it's friendly."

Lightning flashed again and I saw that whatever was coming toward us was moving fast.

"Hey, um, maybe we should go back down to the jail cell," I said, starting to get really nervous about being up here with only the clothes on my back and an orange in my hand.

"Yeah," Karen said, sounding like someone who realized that she might have made a huge mistake by coming up here in the first place. "Maybe you're—"

SLAM!

We turned to see that the door to the stairs had slid shut. The trees had closed up their city and we were about to face their enemy, whether we wanted to or not.

I sure hoped that whatever was heading toward us was afraid of oranges.

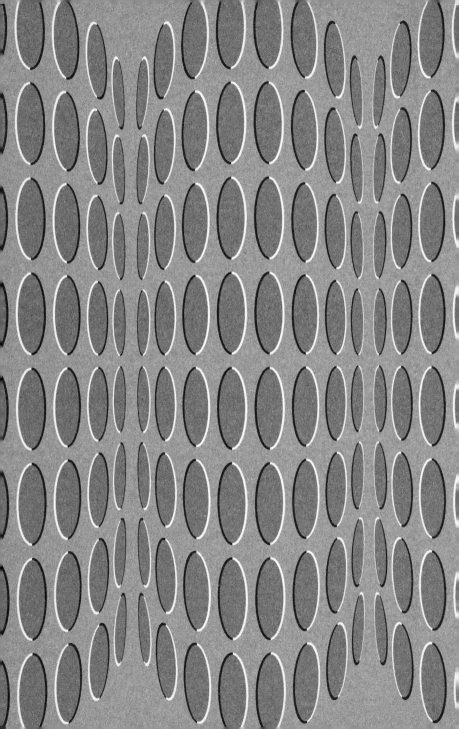

12
Poison Ivy

Bright lights snapped on. Spotlights on top of the battle vehicles pointed through the rain at the approaching enemy and illuminated the battlefield like a rock concert.

And that was when my heart leaped out of my chest.

The rolling field was alive! It was an endless army of killer plants charging toward us at top speed, making a chorus of terrifying clicking and squealing sounds. They were packed together tightly, a rolling tidal wave of leaves and stems and vines and red dandelions like the one that had tried to strangle Karen and me. They were swarming over the tops of each other, leaping up from the pack and throwing themselves forward, like they simply couldn't wait to attack the tree army. Long vines, short vines, spiky leaves, pointy thorns, flowers with teeth, angry ferns—they were all less than thirty seconds away from killing Karen and me about a thousand times.

Whirs and rumbles came from the battle vehicles as their blades began to spin and their claws began to snap and their cables began to whirl like giant weed whackers. All the trees standing in formation grabbed sharp-looking weapons off their belts and prepared for the attack.

Things were about to get extremely ugly.

"We really gotta get out of here," I said to Karen, remembering how bad things had been when we were attacked by just *one* weed.

"It's too late for that," said Yarg's voice through the translator as we felt branches wrap around us and pull us up into the air, making Karen drop her sword. Yarg held us up in front of his angry eye.

"You're as bad as the One Ringers," he said, pointing at the approaching plants. "You never listen."

He then thrust us up into his top branches and let go so that he could use his tree hands to grab more weapons off his belt. Then Yarg started running back to his army.

Holding onto a tree while it's running is a bit like trying not to fall off the monkey bars during an earthquake. Fortunately, Yarg had big enough limbs on his head for us to simply wrap our arms and legs around them and hang on for dear life.

Yarg stopped next to the battle vehicles, raised his deadly-looking sword that had all kinds of hooked blades sticking out of it, and yelled: "FIRST WAVE PREPARE!"

The metal spiders snapped their claws. The tricycles sped up their cables, and the tractor blades whirred faster.

"I don't feel very good," I said to no one in particular as I stared at the bloodthirsty army of plants closing in on us and thought about my comfortable bed back in the frequency I was really wishing I had never left.

"ON MY COMMAND!" Yarg yelled, never taking his eyes off the approaching plants.

Man, he'd better hurry up, I thought to myself, or we're going to be up to our armpits in killer plants.

Yarg swung his sword down like the guy who waves

the green flag at the start of the Indianapolis 500 and creaked a loud "NOW!" just as the plants were about to leap at the vehicles.

Oh, man.

The tractors spun their tires and drove straight into the wall of plants, swinging their blades back and forth like a team of gardeners hacking through a field of tall weeds.

BRAZZZ! The first wave of plants ran right into the blades and went flying everywhere as they were cut to pieces.

The weeds behind them immediately jumped into the air to avoid the blades but the trees quickly lifted the metal arms and the blades chopped the wall of leaping weeds in half too.

Quickly a wave of vines rushed under the raised blades and flew directly at the trees driving the tractors. The vines hit them hard and spun around their trunks like tetherball cords at the end of a game, wrapping tightly around the trees' eyes to blindfold them. But the trees immediately slid long, thin knives up against their bark and cut the vines off as they continued to swing the tractor blades back and forth through the dense swarm of attacking plants.

More vines rushed under the swinging blades and

flew at the tricycles. But the tricycles started spinning in place like tops, becoming tornadoes of whirling cables.

ZAT! The vines hit the cables and exploded into clouds of green clippings as the spinning tricycles rolled closer together to form an impenetrable wall of garden machinery.

The plant army split down the middle and swarmed wide around the spinning tricycles and swinging tractor blades to attack the standing tree army. But the metal spiders intercepted them, snapping their scissor claws wildly into the rushing sea of plants as pieces of stems and leaves flew everywhere. The trees' machines seemed to be slowing down the enormous plant army, but it was clear that their battle vehicles were still way outnumbered.

"Yarg, there's too many of them!" I yelled.

"We've never lost a battle to the One Ringers yet," he said back, sounding insulted that I would think the plants could beat them. He then turned to the tree army, raised his sword, and yelled, "CHOP THEM UP!"

The trees all creaked loudly in unison like a football team before it runs out of the locker room for the big game. Then they raised their swords and charged forward into the sea of plants.

What happened next was total insanity. The trees swung their swords expertly and brought down tons of plants, but thousands of other plants leaped between the swinging swords and went crazy. They wrapped around the unprotected parts of the trees, trying to get at their eyes, but the trees swept blades down their trunks and shaved the plants off like they were shaving off beards. Vines were whipping through the mud like super fast snakes and wrapping around the trees' legs. Before they could pull tightly enough to trip the trees, though, the trees would swing their swords down and cut the vines in half. But just as quickly, other vines would wrap around their legs and try to bring them down.

We heard a loud "Assistance!" come out of the translator. One of the big pine trees about fifty feet in front of us had two vines wrapped tightly around his roots and was starting to lose his balance. Immediately, Yarg grabbed the boomerang off his belt and whipped it at the tree's legs. *SWACK!* The boomerang cut through the vines and flew right between the pine tree's roots, then circled back to Yarg, who snatched it out of the air.

"Whoa!" I yelled, unable to control myself. "Nice shot, Yarg!"

"Iggy, shut up, you idiot!" Karen whispered angrily

at me. I was about to get mad at her for being such a party pooper but then saw why I probably shouldn't have yelled loudly enough to draw any attention.

Two plants on the ground slowly looked up at us, then got scary looks, and sprang into the air. Before Yarg could react, the plants landed in the branches around us and started creeping toward us like cats stalking mice. And we were definitely the mice.

"Oh, man, I really need that sword now," said Karen as the plants made a rattlesnake sound.

"Let me handle this," I said, confident that I was going to be as cool a warrior as Yarg was with his boomerang. I wound up and threw the orange as hard as I could at the plants. They both looked up and watched as the orange flew about five feet over their heads.

"Oh, my God," Karen said as she put her face in her hands, "you throw like such a girl."

And with that, the plants screeched loudly and leaped right at us.

Karen quickly did a kung fu kick at what sort of looked like the world's meanest orchid, but its stem moved out of the way just in time. It then twisted into a loop around her ankle and tried to pull her out of the tree.

"Iggy! Help!" she yelled, as her hands struggled to keep their grip.

Before I could call back to her, the other plant circled its long stem around my waist and then started spinning up my chest like I was a mummy it was trying to wrap. Its snakelike head stopped in front of my face and stared at me with a small angry eye. A scary clicking sound came out of it and I saw a light on the translating machine change colors.

"*Where's our gold?*" the voice hissed out.

Oh, no. Not again.

"We didn't take it!" I yelled.

"Yes, you did," it hissed back.

WHACK!

I heard Karen scream and saw that Yarg had just swung a blade up and cut her orchid's stem in half. Karen almost fell out of the tree from the sudden release but found her footing. The next thing I knew, she reached down to Yarg's belt and pulled off a big hooked blade. The plant around me pulled tight like it was trying to squeeze me to death but Karen quickly swung the blade and chopped off the top of its stem, the sharp edge of her knife just missing my face. The plant's grip went slack and I quickly pulled it off me, completely grossed out.

"The plants think we stole their gold, too," I said to Karen, who was trying to catch her breath. "*Everybody* thinks we stole their gold."

"I don't think that's our biggest problem right now," she said as she looked down at the ground.

Having spotted us, more and more plants were running toward Yarg. They were pointing their leaves and spikes at us as Yarg was swinging weapons with all his branches at them. But there were just too many as they started jumping up onto his limbs and stalking toward Karen and me.

"I NEED BACKUP!" Yarg yelled to his fellow trees as he started pulling at the plants with his branchy fingers.

"YARG! I'M COMING!"

I turned and saw Gree trying to fight her way through the plants. But she now had hundreds of them pulling on her.

The plants in the branches around us moved in closer and closer and we heard them clicking in unison....

"Where's our gold? Where's our gold?"

We were in big trouble.

WHOOSH!

From out of nowhere, Karen and I were grabbed from behind and found ourselves flying through the air.

The palm tree from our prison cell had each of us held tightly in one of his fronds.

"What are you doing?" Karen yelled as the palm tree bounced his roots off the top of a spinning weed whacker and bounded high over the mechanical spider.

"I'm getting you out of here," he said coolly through the translator.

And with that, he landed in the mud next to the battlefield and started hopping us off into the rain and darkness. I heard the trees behind us yelling, "The traitor! He's taking the gold thieves!" I turned around to look at the battle and saw the entire plant army stop fighting the trees and run after us.

"The plants are following us!" I yelled.

"Just calm down and trust me," the palm tree said as he gave me a look. "And quit yelling in my ear."

He then looked at Karen and shook his head at her like he couldn't believe what a wuss I was. She stared at him for a second, then chuckled and made a face back at him like she agreed.

Man, is there any place in the universe where people don't make fun of me?

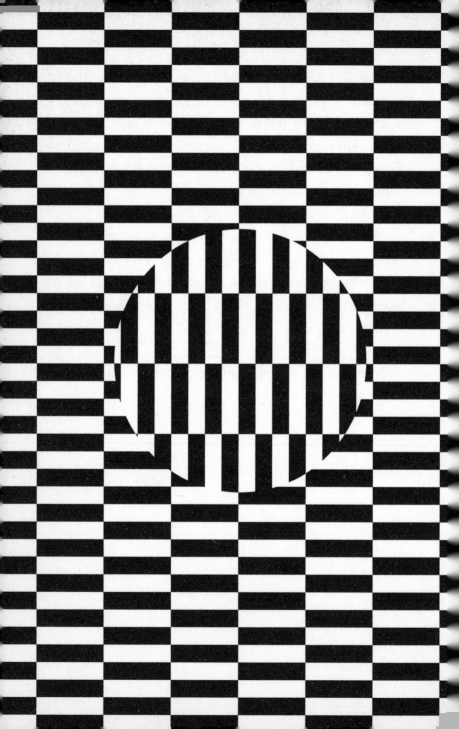

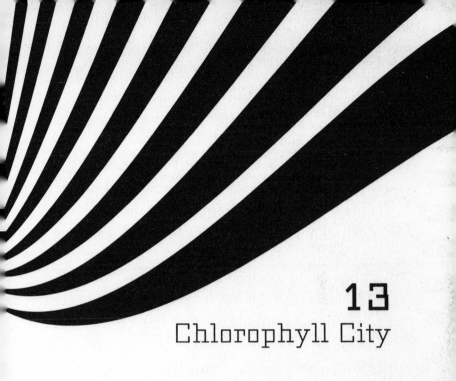

13
Chlorophyll City

I can pretty safely assume you've never been carried by a palm tree that's running across an endless wasteland of mud, and so I'll take this opportunity to describe to you what it feels like:

It doesn't feel good.

When the palm tree ran, he did it like a kangaroo, jumping forward and bouncing off the ground as he propelled himself toward wherever it was we were going. Which meant my body and brain were getting slammed up and down so hard I began to wonder if I'd ever be able to walk again once we finally stopped.

"Karen," I said through the brain-jolting tree bounces, "are you okay?"

"I'm fine," she said with what I had to assume was another roll of her eyes since her tone sounded like she thought my question was annoying. "Why wouldn't I be?"

"Well, I'm glad you are because I think *I'm* going to heave."

"Sorry for the rough ride, Your Highness," the palm tree said super sarcastically. "I had to get you both out of there. In case you couldn't tell, the trees are not your friends."

"Well, neither are the plants," I said, not liking his attitude. "They've tried to kill us like a billion times since we got here."

"Iggy, just be quiet, would you?" Karen said with a sigh.

"Hey, *you* be quiet!" I fired back, losing my cool. "I have no idea what's going on, I'm soaking wet, I feel sick to my stomach, and we're still being chased by a bunch of plants that want to strangle us."

"Don't worry about them," said the palm tree as he hit the ground and took a huge leap forward. "They just think you took their gold."

"You know, I'm tired of getting blamed for something that Herbert Golonski did," I said angrily. "Just because we're humans, everybody assumes that we're the same as he is. That's discrimination, you know. You get in trouble for that back where we're from."

I glanced over at Karen, who gave me a "Didn't I tell you to shut up?" look. Clearly she was trying to look cool in front of this tree who she had some weird crush on and I guess my outbursts were ruining it for her. I just shook my head and tried to see exactly where we were heading. Out of the darkness, lights appeared up ahead, and when I squinted I could see some big glowing structure in the middle of them all. I couldn't be sure but it almost looked like a huge tent.

"Is that your city?" I asked the palm tree, whose name I still didn't know.

"That's the place," he said. "I hope it's up to Your Royal Majesty's high standards."

And with that oh-so-witty zinger, he started bounding even faster toward the city. As he did, the moon came through the clouds and lit up the ground in front of us. And that was when I saw that we were now hopping through what looked like an enormous campground.

There was junk everywhere, like somebody had thrown the world's biggest outdoor party and hadn't bothered to clean it up. Cans and buckets and metal cups were scattered all over the place. And up ahead, in the middle of it all, there actually *was* a tent—a gigantic circus tent.

"Welcome home," the palm tree said as we bounced up to the tent's entrance.

Karen and I exchanged a worried look as the palm pushed through a huge flap and carried us into the tent.

Inside, the noise hit us like we had walked into a rock concert. Tens of thousands of insane plants were screeching and going bananas. They covered every inch of the ground and were running and jumping and fighting and wrestling and leaping onto to the tall poles that were holding up the tent and swinging on trapezes

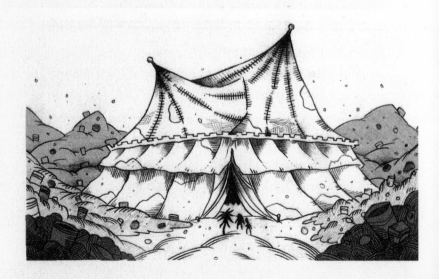

that hung from the ceiling and swarming up and down the walls like cockroaches and it looked and sounded like the craziest place on earth.

The palm tree flexed back so that his trunk stretched like taffy and a loud high-pitched creak came out of him.

"SHUUUUT UUUUUUP!" the palm tree's voice blasted out of the translator.

The plants all stopped what they were doing and went silent so suddenly that it felt like my ears popped and I had gone deaf. They all turned and looked at the palm tree and very quickly saw Karen and me, wrapped in the palm tree's fronds like two little cocktail weenies inside pigs-in-blankets. A wave of angry clicking sounds rippled across the plants as they obviously decided they didn't like Karen and me very much.

"Hey, uh...tree?" I said quietly, not wanting to do anything else to upset the already very upset plants.

"My name's Irk," he said back, sounding slightly annoyed.

"Um...Irk, are the plants going to kill us?" I asked as casually as a person could ask a question containing those particular words in that particular order.

"They'd like to."

"Yeah, I sort of picked up on that," I said as I looked

over at Karen, who tried to give me a "Shut up" look but was clearly as worried as I was with all this deadly greenery surrounding us.

As the plants began to creep toward us and the angry clicking got louder, Irk held up one of his fronds and signaled for the plants to calm down.

"Hey, *KNOCK IT OFF*!" he shouted, as his voice rattled the translator around my neck.

And with that, all the angry clicking stopped.

"Thank you," he said. He then held Karen and me up for all the plants to see and pointed at us. "These guys right here? The ones you want to kill? Well, don't. Because they didn't take our gold. They just come from the same place that the guy who did came from. So back off and leave them alone."

As soon as he said this, the plants all nodded, then turned away from us and went back to what they had been doing moments before, which was going absolutely nuts.

"Wow," Karen said, surprised. "What are you? Like their leader or something?"

"Not officially," Irk shrugged. "They just do everything I tell them to do."

"But you're a tree," I said.

"Yeah, and *you* look like the guy who stole our

gold," he snapped. "Does that mean you're the same as he is?"

"No," I said, a bit intimidated.

"Exactly. So don't ever call me a tree again."

Man, why was everybody in this frequency so grouchy?

14
Meeting
of the Vines

If I had thought this frequency was muggy when we were outside, the air inside the plant city tent was like being underwater. There was no breeze and no air conditioning, and it was pretty clear that the plants liked this temperature and humidity. Unfortunately, I wasn't a plant and so I was sweating like a pig.

Irk had brought us into a smaller tent that was attached to the main one. It seemed like it was some sort of office, although there wasn't any furniture. There were just a bunch of metal poles sticking up out of the ground, as well as some ropes hanging from the ceiling. Irk was leaning against what looked like a metal playground slide that was shaped like a banana. I guess for him it was a chair, although it didn't look particularly comfortable.

Karen and I were sitting on a couple of empty metal buckets we had turned over, which was currently making me lose the circulation in my butt. If I thought the last frequency was devoid of comfortable furniture, it was like a La-Z-Boy showroom compared to this place.

"Trees suck," Irk said as he pulled over a bucket filled with a black liquid and put his feet in it. "That's why I had to get out of that place."

"Why were you in jail?" Karen asked as I stared at the weird black liquid Irk was soaking in.

"Because I defected," he said as he gave Karen a wink. "Do you have any idea what it was like living in the tree city?"

"It didn't seem like a very fun place," I said.

"*Not very fun?*" Irk laughed. "Try 'the most oppressive place on earth.' From the minute you sprout they control your life. Before you can walk or talk, they pull you up and lock you in this huge room with lots of other new sprouts. Then they stand there and lecture to you about what it means to be a tree and how to live in the tree city and yell at you if you do or say anything. This goes on day after day and month after month until you're able to move your roots. And once you can, they lock you in these smaller rooms and don't let you run or play or have fun or do anything except memorize the Book of Rules."

"What's in the Book of Rules?" Karen asked, leaning forward on her bucket.

"What *isn't* in the Book of Rules?" Irk snorted. "Rules are all they care about there. Rules for what you can't do, what you shouldn't do, what you're not allowed to do, what you have to do. Rules about when you can talk and when you *can't* talk, which is pretty much never. Rules against running, jumping, fighting, laughing, eating, drinking, sleeping. Rules for what you should think, who you should like, and who you should hate. And who *they* really hate are the plants. So you can only imagine what the trees think of me for coming over here."

Karen shook her head in disbelief. "When did you leave the tree city?"

"A few rings ago. After spending fifteen rings in the maturity hole, I had to get out of there or I was gonna go nuts."

"The maturity hole?" I asked, thinking whatever that was sounded really weird.

"Yeah, that's where they put you once you've spent two rings memorizing the Book," Irk said, shaking his head in disapproval. "They teach you everything you need to know about tree history and math and science and it wouldn't be so bad except for the fact that it's all really about completely crushing your spirit and making sure that you grow up to be a totally conformist member of their society. To which I said, kiss my trunk."

Irk arched his back like he was taking a deep breath. We heard a sucking sound and saw that the dark liquid he was standing in was going down, like he was taking a big drink through his roots. He made a noise that showed that whatever it was he was drinking was making him feel good. Then he stared at both of us like he was trying to figure us out.

"Now," Irk said as he leaned forward, "I need to ask *you* guys a few ques—"

Just then, the door flap flew open and three plants

walked in. They were the first plants I had seen since I got here that weren't running or going crazy. One was a really tall sunflower with a stem that was thick and rough looking and leaves that were long and muscular. In the middle of its big sunflower face was a huge eye with an angry look that let the world know this sunflower wasn't happy. Behind it was a very thin vine that was half as tall as the sunflower and had droopy leaves that didn't look particularly healthy. Little prickly thorns were sticking out under its eye, which made it look like a guy who hadn't shaved for a few days. Following behind the vine was a short, fat plant that looked like an oversized artichoke. It walked uncomfortably on two thick stumpy stems and I got the feeling that if it had a choice it would simply stand in one place all day and never move.

"Irk, what are you doing?" the sunflower asked in a deep and angry voice as he walked up in front of Karen and me and looked us over, his eyebrow furrowing like he disapproved of us in a major way. "Are you crazy bringing more meat here? Wasn't Herbert bad enough?" He then bent way down and stared right into Karen's face, inches from her nose. Never a good idea.

"You've got two seconds to get out of my face or I'll

pop your head off like a dandelion," she said in a low growl.

The sunflower looked surprised, then stared at the translator hanging around my neck. He stood up and turned to Irk.

"He's wearing the Golonski talking machine!" the sunflower said, pointing at the disc around my neck. "How can you say they weren't involved?!"

"Because they weren't," Irk countered, giving the sunflower a look that said "Don't ever question me again."

The sunflower stared at Irk, then threw his leaves

in the air like he wasn't at all happy about not getting a better explanation. "Fine. You know best. Clearly you're smarter than I am."

"Dirt is smarter than you," the thin vine said under his breath, which made the artichoke burst out laughing.

The sunflower turned and grabbed one of the artichoke's spiky leaves, yanking him up off the ground.

"Something funny, fat boy?"

"All right, *enough!*" Irk said impatiently as he took his roots out of the now empty bucket of black liquid and pushed it aside. "Just introduce yourselves to our guests."

The sunflower gave Irk another long stare to show that saying hello to us was the last thing in the world he wanted to do. Then he turned to us, glared, and said, "I'm Hoosh, head of the army and *eliminator of all thieves and traitors*," making sure to drive home the last part of his introduction so we wouldn't miss it.

The vine rolled his eye again, then gave us a small unenthusiastic wave with one of his limp leaves. "I'm Shushle. Minister of culture, although this place wouldn't know something cultural if it bit it in the stem."

Karen and I looked at the artichoke, who stared back at us blankly for a second, then looked confused, like he didn't really think he would have to talk to us. "Oh. Um, I'm Choonk. I'm just friends with Shushle."

"He's in charge of the games," Shushle said with a shake of his head. "But he hasn't really done much yet."

"I've got a lot going on," Choonk said with a shrug as Shushle rolled his eye again, clearly a bit fed up with his chunky friend. "I'm very busy."

"Okay, now you know who we are," Hoosh the sunflower said impatiently. "Now, who are *you* and why is Irk so sure that you don't work with Herbert Golonski?"

Karen gave Hoosh a dirty look, then turned to me and said, "Iggy, just tell him, would you? I can't keep repeating this story."

As Shushle and Choonk both got buckets of the dark liquid and put their roots in them, I told them all about the last frequency we were in and about Herbert and the frequency transporter and the stolen gold. They seemed pretty surprised at the whole frequency thing, which I guess *is* pretty surprising the first time you hear about it. But when I told them about how Herbert did the same thing to the trees and walked off with all their gold, Hoosh suddenly got angry and kicked over an empty bucket next to him.

"Okay, this is a total scam," he said as he turned to Irk. "Don't you see that we're being set up? The trees had these two meats tell this story in front of you and then they let you escape when we attacked so that you'd bring their story back here and we'd think they were innocent and that they didn't have our gold. That is the weakest plan ever. And I can't believe you fell for it!"

Irk stared at Hoosh like he was about to beat him up, then suddenly looked like he had decided maybe Hoosh was right. As his eye stared at me accusingly, I began to feel like maybe I *had* made the whole story up, even though I hadn't. It was like when your mom is so convinced that you broke something you know you didn't break that you start to wonder if maybe you actually *did* break it.

Irk stared at Karen, who stared back at him the same way she had when they had their showdown in our jail cell. The whole room was quiet, even though the sound of the insane plant party in the main tent was leaking into the room through the canvas walls.

Finally, Irk broke his stare with Karen. He turned to Hoosh.

"Their story's true. We're finished talking."

Hoosh shook his head, grunted, and stalked away.

And that was when the door flap flew open and a hurricane spun into the room.

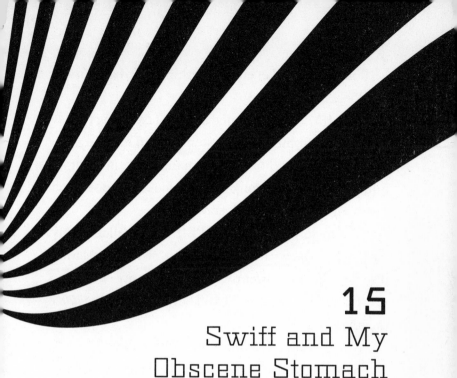

15
Swiff and My Obscene Stomach

Okay, it wasn't a hurricane. But it might as well have been.

A daisy about as tall as Karen came spinning into the room, then did a somersault through the air and landed on Hoosh's shoulders, draping its long stem around him like a scarf. It then put its daisy face in front of his eye and said at about a million miles an hour, "Hoosh! Hoosh! Where's the meat?! Where's the meat?!"

Before he could even say anything, the daisy turned and looked right at me.

"It's HIM!" she screamed and the next thing I knew she flew at me and spun her stem around my body like a boa constrictor, her face stopping right in front of mine. Her eye went huge and she looked like she had just seen her favorite rock star.

"You're so CUUUUUUTE!!!" she yelled in my face as her voice came muffled out of the translating disc that she was currently crushing into my chest.

"I...can't...breathe," I said because, well, I *couldn't* breathe.

"Swiff!" yelled Hoosh. "Get off him! *Now!*"

She quickly unwrapped herself off me like fishing line coming off a reel and leaped back onto Hoosh's shoulders.

"Can I have him? Can I have him?" she said in Hoosh's face.

"Swiff, get out of here," he said back to her sternly. "Go drive someone else crazy, would you?"

"I want him to be my boyfriend! Can he be my boyfriend?!"

"Geez," Karen said in disbelief. "Get a grip, chick."

Hearing this, Swiff the daisy flew at Karen and

wrapped around her chest and arms before Karen could even react. This was one fast flower.

"Yeah, and what's it to you, *chick*?" Swiff said angrily, about an inch from Karen's face. Karen's brow furrowed and we could all see that she was about one millisecond away from headbutting Swiff right in the eye. Luckily, Hoosh threw out his longest leaf and yanked Swiff off of Karen.

"Psycho flower touches me again and she's mulch, you hear me?" Karen yelled at Hoosh, clenching her fists.

Swiff struggled to break free from Hoosh's grip and attack Karen again but Hoosh walked over to the flap, opened it, and threw Swiff back out into the big tent.

"Sorry about that," Irk said with a sigh. "Hoosh's sister is a bit...overenthusiastic."

"Gee, you think?" Karen said sarcastically as she straightened her shirt.

I looked over at Hoosh to see what he was going to say next and it was at that very moment my stomach chose to do something really embarrassing. It growled. But it wasn't one of those quiet growls that sound like a creaky little door. It was a really loud one, which apparently sounded like some word in plant language because all of a sudden a super obscene insult came out of the translating disc.

Hoosh's eye stared at me in shock, and then he looked really mad.

"What did you just call me?" he asked as he began to stalk forward, the ends of his leaves balled into fists.

"I didn't call you anything!" I said in a panic. "My stomach just growled!"

"Nobody's ever called me that and lived," he said as he kept walking toward me.

"But I didn't mean it! It was my stomach!"

"It really wasn't cool to call him that," Irk said.

"But I *didn't say it*!" I yelled.

"Was that really your stomach?" Karen asked, giving me an extremely weird look.

"OF COURSE IT WAS!" I hollered, my voice cracking, which made the word *course* come out two octaves higher than the other words around it. "I would never call anybody something like that."

"Your *stomach* swears in plant language?" she said with a shake of her head. "Just when I thought you couldn't get weirder."

Hoosh walked up and was about to grab me by the

collar when Karen stepped in front of me and stared him down.

"Touch him and you'll be missing a lot of leaves, stretch," she said scarily.

Hoosh looked back at Irk for help. Irk leaned forward in his chair and said, "What's a stomach and why would it say things you can't control?"

"A stomach is where our food goes when we eat and it makes noise when we *don't* eat," she said calmly. "And Iggy and I haven't eaten for a long time."

The plants all exchanged looks like they were trying to figure out whether to believe her or not.

"Hey, man, everybody's gotta eat," Shushle said to the group with a shrug.

"There's some food right over there," Irk said, pointing to some piles of dirt in the corner.

"Thanks, but we don't eat dirt," said Karen.

"You want some dark?" Shushle asked as he held up a bucket of the stinky black liquid and put it under our noses.

"We'll pass," Karen said in the raspy voice you get when you try to talk while you're holding your breath.

"No dark? No dirt? What *do* you eat?" asked Choonk.

Karen and I both looked at Choonk, the giant talking artichoke, and I'm pretty sure we both realized at the same moment that if we had a huge pot of boiling water to put Choonk in for twenty minutes, he'd be pretty delicious.

"Uh...why're you guys looking at me like that?" Choonk asked nervously as he slowly stepped behind Shushle.

Karen glanced at me like she didn't really know how to address their question about what we eat. How exactly are you supposed to tell your hosts that back in your world you usually eat many of them?

"Well, if you're hungry, let's go take a look around," Irk said, getting up from his chair. "But I'm starting to think you might just have to learn to enjoy dirt and dark."

Man, I really should have held on to that orange.

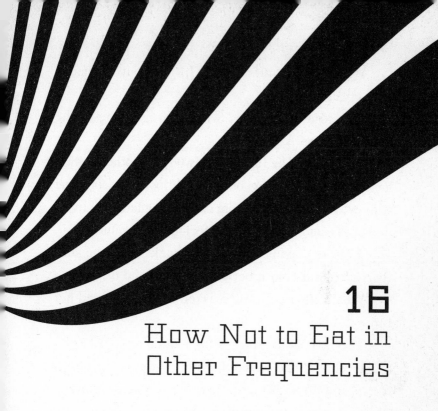

16
How Not to Eat in Other Frequencies

We stepped through the flap that separated the small room from the big tent. The sound of thousands of crazy plants hit us again, but there was definitely something different going on. The plants' attention seemed to be focused on something happening in the center of the tent. They were blocking our view; they all climbed on top of each other to see better, cheering and generally going wild.

"What's going on?" I asked Irk as I put my hands over my ears.

"Who knows?" he said with a shrug. "One of the games, I guess. Ask Choonk."

Karen and I looked at Choonk, who got another worried look on his face. I guess once you've looked at someone with eyes that tell him you're considering having him for dinner, it's hard for him to ever feel relaxed around you.

"They're playing Bucket," Choonk said as he subtly tried to put Hoosh between himself and us.

"What's Bucket?" Karen asked as she furrowed her brow.

"Take a look," said Irk, who nodded to Hoosh.

Hoosh grabbed Karen and me by the backs of our collars and lifted us up to see over the wall of jumping plants. There in the middle of the tent were about fifty plants chasing a bucket around. They'd knock it away from one plant, then a bunch of them would all swarm after the bucket and practically kill each other to get ahold of it. As soon as one of them did, another bunch of plants would crash into the plant with the bucket and the bucket would go flying again.

"How do they score points?" I asked, although my voice sort of sounded like a frog because my shirt was cutting into my Adam's apple.

"Points?" Choonk said, confused. "What do you mean?"

"How do you win?" Karen asked as she stared at the plants that were currently in a huge dog pile trying to get the bucket.

"If you get the bucket, you win," Choonk said as if Karen and I were total idiots.

"Does anyone ever really get the bucket?" I asked as I saw more plants rush into the game and dive into the pile.

Choonk looked at Shushle, who stared back at him.

"I don't know." Shushle shrugged. "Everybody usually loses interest before that ever happens."

Right at that moment, the bucket popped up out of the pile and flew toward us. The plants in front of us all leaped up to grab it and a huge riot broke out.

"Do you have any games that are a little more… organized?" I asked as a bunch of plants fell against the tent wall next to us and started beating the crap out of each other while they all tugged on the bucket.

"Organized?" Choonk said like he had never heard the word. "I don't know. We also play Can."

"What's that?" Karen asked.

"Well, there's a can and everybody tries to grab it."

"That's sounds the same as Bucket."

"It's totally not," Choonk said, sounding insulted. "Instead of a bucket, you use a can."

Karen gave him one of her looks that showed she thought Choonk was lame and said, "Any other games that are different?"

"Um…" Choonk said as he looked at Shushle for help.

"There's Bucket Can," Shushle said proudly.

"Let me guess," said Karen. "You chase a bucket *and* a can at the same time."

Choonk and Shushle stared at her for a few seconds, then both said "Yeah" in unison.

"Wow," was all Karen said as she shook her head like she had just decided that the plant city was the dumbest place she'd ever been.

"You should play soccer," I said as the idea suddenly dawned on me.

"What's that?" Choonk asked.

"You split into two teams of eleven players each, then you set up goals at both ends of the field, then each team kicks the ball…or bucket…down the field as the other team tries to stop them, and if you kick the bucket into the other team's goal, you get one point. And when one hour is up, whoever has the most points wins."

Choonk and Shushle stared at me.

"That's it?" Shushle asked.

"Yeah," I said. "Well, except that you're not allowed to use your hands at all."

Choonk looked perplexed. "Huh?"

"You have to kick it back and forth to each other and at the goal. The only person who's allowed to use his hands is the goalie, who tries to stop the bucket from going into the goal. Anybody else who touches the bucket with their hands gets a penalty from a guy called the 'referee.'"

Choonk and Shushle exchanged another look as they thought about what I had told them.

"Um...okay, whatever," Choonk finally said like he thought I had just presented the lamest idea he had ever heard.

Yeah, and soccer's only the most popular sport in the world, I thought. Whatever yourself, you stupid artichoke.

"C'mon," Irk said to Karen. "Let's go take a look out back."

We started walking again and passed an opening that led into another small side room. I peeked inside...

And I almost fainted.

There in the center of the room was a big pit that

was filled with fruit—strawberries, blueberries, raspberries, blackberries, green grapes, red grapes. The fruit was colorful and perfect looking, like it was the freshest fruit in the world, and all just sitting there waiting to be eaten.

"Karen," I said as I tapped her on the arm. "Food!"

I saw her eyes light up as she looked at the smorgasbord in front of us. Overcome by hunger, I ran into the room, grabbed two huge handfuls of berries, and stuffed them into my mouth. The flavor practically exploded on my tongue and I almost started crying because the fruit was the best I'd ever had. My dad used to drive to the farms outside of the town where we lived to buy fresh berries during harvest time and I could never believe how good they were. Well, these berries in the pit were about a hundred times better than those.

As I chewed with my mouth stuffed so full of berries that I must have looked like the world's greediest chipmunk, I looked next to me to see if Karen was also eating. But she wasn't there. I turned and looked back at the opening to see where she was.

And that was when I stopped eating.

Irk, Hoosh, Choonk, and Shushle were standing in

the doorway next to Karen, just staring at me. Behind them were a bunch of plants that all had shocked looks on their faces. And right at the top of the doorway was Swiff, who was sitting on Hoosh's shoulders, her eye wide in horror.

"Ew, gross!" she yelled like she was about to throw up. "He's eating our *seeds*!"

And with that, all the plants went nuts. Some of them started laughing like crazy, others started to gag, and others just continued to stare at me in shock.

"Oh, man, I think I'm going to barf," said Shushle.

I gave Karen what I'm sure was a pretty helpless

look, being that I was now completely embarrassed. "Help me out here, would you, Karen?"

Karen's eyes were definitely wide at the sight of all the fruit in the pit, and I could tell her hunger was winning over her constant desire to accuse me of doing something wrong.

"Look, everybody," Karen said, sounding a bit unsure of what exactly she should say as she turned to address all the plants. "Where we're from, we eat what's in that pit."

The plants went even more nuts, screaming and laughing and gagging and falling all over each other. Which clearly was making Karen mad.

"Hey, just calm down, would you?" she said impatiently. "I'm trying to tell you that everything's different where we're from. Like in our world, plants don't talk or walk or run or do anything except grow in the dirt."

But it was no use. The plants were too busy telling other plants about what Karen said and about what I was eating and pretty soon we heard the whole circus tent going crazy about the two "meats" who were so disgusting that they ate "seeds" out of "the pit."

"You know what?" Karen said, turning to me, fed up. "I'm hungry and I'm eating." She then turned back to Irk and the gang and said, "Deal with it." Then she pulled the flap shut on them, walked over to the pit, and sat down next to me.

"So much for trying to look cool," she said with a shake of her head.

"Hey, what do I care?" I shrugged. "I guess this frequency will just be one more place where people make fun of me."

"Yeah." Karen popped a big red grape into her mouth. "I never fit in anywhere either. So, why start now?"

And with that, Karen and I dug into what I guess was the plant city toilet and had the best meal we'd had since we met.

17
I Become a Big Shot

Apparently neither Karen nor I knew just how tired we were.

But we must have been *really* tired because the last thing I remembered was stuffing our faces with berries and grapes. The next thing I knew I woke up feeling like I had slept a really long time. I felt rested but had a bit of a headache and my stomach sort of hurt. I felt the same way I always did the morning after Halloween, when instead of rationing out my pillowcase full of candy, I would instead eat pretty much all of it in one night and then fall asleep in what my dad used to call a "sugar coma."

Karen was still sound asleep on the ground next to me. I guess I probably would have still been asleep too, but the noise outside the pit room pulled me out of my dreams like a pair of tweezers yanking a splinter out of my finger. I stood up slowly so I wouldn't wake Karen and then went through the flap to take a look at what was going on.

At first it looked like the plants were all just watching another stupid game of Bucket. But when I climbed onto a post to see just how many of them were beating each other up, I saw something I never expected to see in a million years.

They were playing soccer.

They had cleared out the center area of the tent and set up goals on each end with goalies guarding them. Ten of them were kicking the bucket back and forth as they made their way down the field while another ten of them tried to steal the bucket and kick it down to the other end. And even though the field wasn't really the right size and the goals were too big, it actually looked like a real game of soccer.

Just then, a plant scored a goal. The crowd screamed, and started going so crazy that it seemed like soccer was about the greatest thing they had ever seen. And that was when somebody saw me and yelled, "IT'S *HIM*!"

Every plant under the Big Top turned and looked at me. Fully expecting to have the entire audience start yelling "Seed eater!" I tried to jump down from the post so I could get the heck out of there. But before I could, a bunch of plants swarmed underneath me and hoisted me into the air like I was some kind of hero. They started passing me all around the tent and then down to the playing field while they patted me on the back, shouting things like "You're the greatest!" and "We love your game!" and "You are the coolest meat who ever lived!"

As freaked out as I was, I have to admit that I was sort of enjoying all the attention. I mean, hey, I've never been popular in my life. And so having tens of thousands of plants inside a giant circus tent cheer for me pretty much ranked as a high point in my life.

"Put him down! Put the meat down!" Choonk yelled as he pushed his way through the crowd and pulled me down.

He then grabbed my hand and held my arm up over

my head like I had just won a boxing match. "Behold, the inventor of Iggy Bucket!" Choonk yelled as the crowd cheered.

"No, wait," I said to Choonk. "That game you're playing's called soccer."

"No, it's not," he said back loud enough for everyone to hear. "This game is called Iggy Bucket. After the meat who invented it."

"But I didn't invent it," I said.

However, the crowd was cheering so loudly they couldn't hear me.

"I mean, it's a really popular game back where I'm from."

"What other games can you teach us?" Choonk asked loudly as the crowd suddenly quieted down, waiting to hear what I'd say next.

"Um…" I stammered, now feeling nervous to have the entire plant city hanging on my every word. "I don't know. I mean, there's football, baseball, basketball, volleyball—"

"Teach us how to play them, O Great Meat Master of Games!" Choonk said really loudly so the crowd could hear him.

"Yes!" the crowd yelled. Then they started chanting

in unison, "Teach us more games, O Great Meat Master! Teach us more games, O Great Meat Master!"

And since they wouldn't shut up and since they really did seem to want to know more games, I did just that. I told them the basic rules of all the games I knew, even though I hardly knew anything about sports, and I drew them the shapes of the different playing fields and equipment. I drew baseball diamonds and football fields and basketball courts and volleyball nets and baseball bats and goal posts and basketball hoops and then I even drew hockey rinks and tennis courts and boxing rings and basically downloaded everything I knew about sports, which was very little. By the time I had finished telling them everything I knew about the world of sports, they were all dead silent.

And then they went nuts.

"Let us see! Let us see the drawings!" the plants all started yelling.

Tons of them tried to run down to get a close-up look at the diagrams I had drawn. They were jumping over each other and pushing and fighting and it was like a huge tidal wave of battling plants heading toward us.

Choonk yelled to the soccer players on the field, "Guard the sacred texts!"

"You guys, I can just draw them again if you want," I said, trying to calm them down. But nobody heard me.

There was so much pandemonium from all sides that I thought I was going to get crushed in the middle of it. But just as the fight was closing in on me, Swiff the crazy daisy jumped out of nowhere and wrapped her stem around my chest.

"You want me to get you out of here?" she asked excitedly as she stuck her eye right in my face.

"Yes, please!" I said, completely freaked out by everything around me, including her.

"You got it, boyfriend!"

And with that, she jumped off me and started pushing plants out of the way. I'd seen Karen fight her way through things before but at least Karen had some sort of method to her kung fu. Swiff was just lashing out with every part of her body like a one-flower wrecking machine.

But I have to say, she was definitely getting us through the crowd.

When she finally got us to the outer edge of the tent, she wrapped her stem around my chest again and shoved her eye right into my face.

"I saved you!" she yelled happily. "Now you *have* to be my boyfriend!"

"I thought you said I was gross because I eat seeds," I said, completely freaked out by her.

"You *are* but you're so good looking I don't care!" she shouted as her stem tightened around my ribs. "*And* I know you're super smart now, too! You're the Great Meat Master of Games! HEY, YOU PETAL DROPPERS! MY BOYFRIEND IS THE GREAT MEAT MASTER OF GAMES!"

I turned and saw a bunch of other daisies glaring at us.

Swiff was glaring back at them and moving her head from side to side like she was taunting them.

"Why don't you get your wilty stem off him?" yelled the tallest daisy, who was standing in front of the others. "I mean, he doesn't look like he likes you."

"Oh, yeah?" Swiff said like she was getting ready for a fight. "If he doesn't like me, then how come he's my boyfriend?"

The other daisies started walking toward us like a gang and I immediately started to get nervous. "Just 'cause you say he's your boyfriend," said the tall daisy, "doesn't *make* him your boyfriend."

Swiff slowly unwrapped from around me and stepped forward so that she was eye to eye with her enemy. "Well, I know he ain't your boyfriend because he doesn't like stinkweeds." The tall daisy's eye narrowed as the other daisies around her all went "Oooooh." And the flower girl fight was on.

The other daisies started screaming and cheering as Swiff and her opponent grabbed each other and rolled around on the ground, pulling each other's petals and trying to pin the other one down.

"Stop it, you guys!" I yelled. I'd seen girls get in fights at my school and some of their battles were pretty brutal, but nothing could compare to the fury of this. I stepped forward to try and break them up but as soon as I reached in, one of the other daisies tackled me, landing on my chest.

"Hey, Meat Master," she said scarily as she got

about half an inch from my nose, "You wanna be *my* boyfriend?"

Before I could process the fact that for some reason I seemed to be the Brad Pitt of the plant world, Swiff came flying through the air and landed on the daisy's back. "You want a piece of me too, skank stem?" Swiff yelled as the other daisies all jumped on top of her and started brawling, with me at the bottom of the pile.

"*IGGY!*"

The yell was so loud and angry that all the daisies immediately stopped fighting and looked back at the voice.

Karen was standing next to Irk, staring like she had just caught me peeing into a bowl of soup.

"What are you *doing*?" she asked incredulously, clearly certain that the entire daisy fight was my fault.

"I was just standing here and everybody started fighting over me," I said defensively as my voice cracked.

"Irk needs to talk to us and you've got the translating disc," she said, rolling her eyes. "So, move it, lover boy."

I untangled myself from the mess of daisy stems as Swiff jumped up and shot Karen an angry look. Then she turned to me and said, "See you later...*boyfriend*," and strutted confidently off into the crowd.

"What have you gotten yourself into now?" Karen asked as we headed to Irk's office.

"Nothing," I said innocently. "I didn't do anything."

"Thanks again, O Great Meat Master of Games!" Choonk yelled from the middle of the tent. Karen gave me another look as we walked through the flap into Irk's room.

"For some reason," she said, "I don't believe you."

Yeah, it *was* pretty hard to believe.

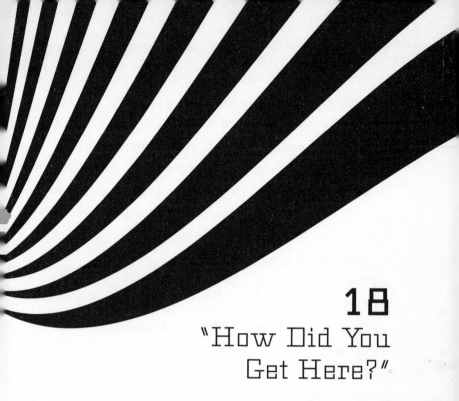

18
"How Did You Get Here?"

"Excuse me?" Karen said as she leaned forward to hear Irk, who was speaking quieter than he usually did.

"I want to know exactly how you got here," Irk said again, his voice even lower this time.

"Why are you talking so quietly?" Karen asked as we both sat cross-legged on the ground in front of Irk, who was in his banana-shaped chair, looking a lot less comfortable than he did before.

"Because I still don't know if you're working with

Herbert or not," he said. "And if it turns out you are, the plants will tear you apart."

"You said you believed us!" Karen yelled, which made Irk jump up out of his chair and get in her face.

"I said that because I didn't want you to get killed," he whispered angrily. Irk then grabbed his side and groaned, as if some enormous pain had seized his body.

"Are you all right?" I asked.

"I'm fine, I'm fine," he said impatiently. "Just tell me how you got here."

"You heard what we told Yarg," Karen said, just as impatient. "Herbert double-crossed us and sent us here to get rid of us. You think we'd be in this stupid world if it was our choice?"

"But you knew how to operate a transporter."

"No, we didn't," Karen said, getting up as if she was ready to storm out of the room. "Iggy did something that turned it on. But it was all a setup that Herbert tricked us into."

Irk stopped and stared at me seriously.

"But you figured out how to turn it on?" he asked.

"Uh…" I stammered, not having thought I was going to be an active part of this conversation. "I guess. I mean, I did what I thought Herbert had done and it started up. But like Karen said, he might have just set it so that it was going to turn on no matter what I did."

Irk kept staring at me, which was making me really uncomfortable, since for all I knew I had a big booger hanging out of my nose that no one had told me about.

"But you *did* turn it on?"

I shrugged my shoulders and said, "Yeah, I guess so."

"Why are you asking him that?" Karen asked as she pulled her hair back behind her ear.

Irk got up and looked out the flap into the main tent. Then he turned back to us.

"Because I think I might know where there's a transporter."

Karen and I exchanged looks of major surprise as my heart sort of skipped a beat.

"Wait a minute," Karen said as she stepped toward Irk and lowered her voice. "Are you serious?"

"I think so. But I don't know for sure."

"Well, where do you think it is?" Karen asked like someone was about to tell her a juicy secret.

"It's in a bad place," Irk said, sounding nervous for the first time since I'd met him. "And the bad place is in the middle of an even worse place."

"Worse than what?" I asked, knowing that wherever that bad place was, there was a good chance Karen and I were going to end up in it.

"Worse than anything you've seen so far," he said with a rather sarcastic snort.

"How do you know about this?" Karen asked.

"It's where Herbert took the gold to," he said, his tone telling us that this was an unpleasant story for him. "Our toughest fighters and I escorted him into the Good Times Ravine, where we transported the gold through the Happy Flats and into the heart of the Life is Beautiful Forest."

"Wait a minute," Karen said, shaking her head like

she couldn't believe what she'd just heard. "Those are supposed to be *bad* places with names like that?"

"The worst," Irk said seriously, giving her a look that said he couldn't believe she would doubt him. "And then after getting past all the dangers that the ravine threw our way, we were suddenly ambushed at the entrance to the Cave of Smiles. I was immediately knocked unconscious and when I woke up none of my fighters were alive. I saw from the marks on the ground that all the gold had been dragged inside the cave and the footprints of Herbert's army disappeared into it also. But when I tried to enter the cave, something happened."

Irk took a deep breath like he was trying not to throw up or something. He looked like he was getting sick just thinking about whatever it was that happened to him.

"Was it something gross?" I asked, almost afraid to hear what he was remembering. I've always been pretty squeamish when it comes to gross things and I even fainted in science class once when they made us dissect an earthworm (which resulted in me getting called "Wussy the Worm Fainter" for the rest of the semester).

Irk took another breath and continued.

"As I approached the mouth of the cave, my trunk

suddenly started to tingle. I figured it was just the after-effects of being knocked unconscious. But as I moved forward, my leaves suddenly started to constrict and it felt like someone had wrapped my body in ropes and was pulling them tighter and tighter. I tried to keep moving but my roots started to harden, like they were turning into stone. And then the inside of my chest felt like it was being twisted by an invisible hand. I tried to speak but couldn't even get out so much as a creak. The next thing I knew, my vision started to go black.

"I knew that if I were to pass out in the mouth of the cave, whatever was causing me to feel that way would probably kill me. And so with the last bit of strength I had, I stumbled away from the cave and somehow got back here, where I passed out and apparently lay unconscious for weeks. How I didn't die, I have no idea."

"It sounds like you were poisoned or something," said Karen as she stared at Irk, concerned.

"Something like that," said Irk. "All the plants think it's a curse. Occasionally, some of them will break off and go to the ravine but they never come back. The Good Times Ravine is a dangerous place for plants, with or without a cursed cave."

"And that's where the transporter is?" Karen asked,

sounding excited about a possible way out of this frequency but also worried about what we'd have to go through to find it.

"It has to be," said Irk as he tried to bring himself out of his weird mood. "If what you say about how you got here is true."

"It's true, all right," said Karen as she stood up, looking ready for action. "So...how do we get to this place?"

Yeah, I was afraid she was going to ask that.

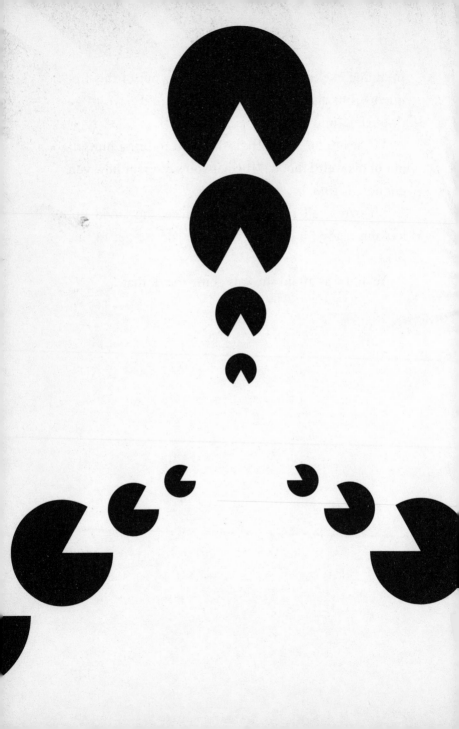

19
The Trip I Didn't
Really Want to Take

We were walking through mud. Again.

And, yes, it was raining too.

Woo hoo.

I had originally hoped when Irk said the ravine was far away that we were going to get another bumpy-yet-no-effort-on-our-behalf ride, courtesy of his powerful leaping abilities. But when he walked out of his room carrying two huge metal canisters filled with dark I had a sinking feeling that we were gonna be what my grandma used to call "hoofin' it."

And so we were as we trudged across the muddy plain toward some ravine I couldn't see, Karen and I each carrying a bucket filled with berries while the thunder rumbled over our heads.

"If this place we're going is so dangerous, how come we're not bringing any weapons?" Karen asked.

"We've *got* weapons," Irk said, glancing at his fronds.

"You're gonna protect us with cans of dark?" I asked, confused.

"No," Irk said as he stopped and set down his cans. "Here's how we're going to protect ourselves." And with that, he went into some elaborate routine of spinning and punching that seemed to be this frequency's version of a kung fu demonstration.

As Irk went through his moves, I saw Karen was watching him with a look that said she really thought he was cool. It was the same look I'd seen girls in our school get when they were watching Todd Barrett, the high school varsity running back, make some amazing play and score a touchdown.

I, on the other hand, thought that Irk looked kind

of goofy as he spun around and chopped at the air like he was getting attacked by bees. It felt kind of show-offy, like when someone starts singing out of nowhere and you have to sit there and pretend you're enjoying it when all you really want them to do is shut up. Karen set down her berry bucket, walked over, and started to copy what Irk was doing, trying to learn his moves. At first, Irk looked surprised by this. But as Karen got better and better, he started to speed up, the two of them locking eyes as he seemed to communicate silently to her what move he was going to do next.

Pretty soon, the two of them were doing the kung fu routine in perfect unison, like they were dance partners on some TV show. As weird as the moment was, there was something kind of cool about it. Especially since the better Karen got at kung fu the more I knew she could protect me, since I had no fighting skills whatsoever.

"Iggy," Irk called out. "Get over here and join us."

"Uh…" I said as my heart sank. "That's okay. You guys are way too good at it."

"That's why you need to do it," Karen said as she spun and kicked out high, sending a deadly spray of mud shooting off her boot. "I'm not going to keep getting you out of trouble all the time."

"It's easy, kid," Irk called over. "You just have to imagine you're like the water that's flowing around our feet. If someone comes at you to attack, you don't hit them head-on. You flow around them and use their strength against them. Like this."

Irk pretended to dodge some invisible attacker running toward him and then spun and pushed his fronds out as if he were shoving the attacker in the back, which would have sent him or her flying.

"Iggy, get your lazy butt over here *now*," Karen yelled with a bit of a smirk, as if she found my discomfort with the whole situation funny.

Feeling stupid, I set down my bucket of berries and walked over to join them. At first, it was like trying to figure out how to jump into a moving jump rope. But once I did jump in...well...it was pretty embarrassing.

"How do you know how to do this?" I asked Karen, as I flailed around like someone had just put ice cubes down the front of my pants.

"I used to take kung fu classes after school. Well, until my dad said it wasn't the kind of thing that girls should be doing and stopped paying for it. He had a pretty old-fashioned view of women."

"What do you mean by 'old-fashioned'?" Irk asked as he kicked the bottom of his trunk up into the air and did a fast spin that made him look like a whirling drill bit.

"Where we're from," said Karen as she somehow did the same move that Irk just did, "women get treated

differently than men. It's getting better but some guys from my dad's generation still have a problem with women doing things like kung fu. They'd rather we just walk around in high heels and laugh at their jokes and do what they tell us to do. But you know what I say to that?"

Karen crouched and spun, doing a leg sweep and knocking my feet out from under me, causing me to fall onto the wet ground.

"OW!" I yelled as the back of my pants got soaked. "What'd you do *that* for?!"

"Oops, sorry, Ig," she said as she reached out to help me up. "I get a little crazy when I talk about that stuff."

"A *little*?" I said as she yanked me to my feet. "I'm not the one who's mean to women. Don't take it out on me."

"C'mon," Karen said with a laugh, "just let us show you a few basic moves in case you need them in the ravine and then we can get going."

I gave her a nod and the three of us got in a circle and started doing different punches and kicks while we pretended to sidestep attacks.

And, amazingly, I started to feel good about what I was doing. I'm sure I looked pretty dumb doing it, but

I was starting to feel like I might now have a couple of moves if I found myself in some hairy situation.

As we continued our routine and began to speed it up, I suddenly felt something next to me.

I turned and saw Swiff the daisy at my shoulder, happily doing our moves as she stared at me with her big daisy eye.

"Ahh!" I screamed, completely shocked to see her.

"Hi there, boyfriend!" she said.

Irk and Karen saw her and immediately stopped.

"Swiff!" Irk yelled. "What are you doing here?"

"I followed you guys," she said like she was sure we were all thrilled to see her. "You're gonna need my help."

"You don't even know what we're doing," Irk said as he threw his fronds in the air.

"You're going to the ravine," she said, her stem bouncing like a spring with excitement.

Irk stared at her. "How do you know that?"

"I heard you guys talking about it when you were in your office," she said cheerily.

"You were *spying* on us?" Irk yelled.

"No, I was just listening in," Swiff said innocently. "I always do."

"You always spy on me in my office?!"

"No, I just always listen in. It's fun."

"Then you're spying on me!" Irk exploded. "And it's not fun! It's against the rules."

"What rules?" she asked, confused.

"The rules that..."

Irk suddenly trailed off and I realized that after seeing the way things worked in the plant city, there was a good chance that there simply were no rules. "Just go back," Irk finally said as he turned away from Swiff.

"I can't," she said. "You guys need me."

"No, we don't," said Karen, putting her hands on her hips.

"Iggy does. 'Cause I'm his girlfriend."

"Not really," I said, feeling very caught in the middle.

"Yes, you are!" she yelled as she quickly spun around me and got in my face.

Karen and Irk both lunged for her but fortunately Irk grabbed her first, since Karen had a look in her eyes like she was going to play "she loves me/she loves me not" with Swiff's petals.

"I said go back to the city, Swiff!" Irk yelled as he yanked her off of me and marched her in the direction we had just come from. He then set her down firmly onto the ground in a way that said he was dead serious.

Swiff stared at him like she was going to protest, then saw that he was not open to argument.

"I'm telling you, you're gonna need me," she said under her breath as Irk turned and headed back to us. He picked up one of the cans of dark, popped open the lid, stuck a root in, and took a long drink. Then he grimaced and grabbed his side like he was in pain again.

"Are you okay?" I asked.

"Yes, I'm fine," he said, now in a bad mood. "Let's just go."

He picked up the other can and headed off in the direction of the ravine. Karen gave me a look that said she wasn't sure what was going on, shot an angry glance back at Swiff, picked up her bucket of berries, and headed after Irk.

I looked back at Swiff, who was just standing and staring at me. I felt kinda bad, since she seemed hurt that we were all being so mean to her. It's just, well, she *was* sort of annoying and yet she did like me for some reason. And I feel that if somebody likes me, no matter who they are, I should probably like them back.

I gave her a little shrug that was sort of a halfhearted apology, picked up my berries, and ran off after Karen and Irk.

And when I glanced back over my shoulder again, Swiff was gone.

20
Scene at
the Ravine

It was different from any cloud I'd ever seen, either in this frequency or anywhere else I'd been in my life.

In fact, "cloud" isn't really the right word. It looked almost like there was a fire up ahead that was creating a huge purple-and-yellow smoke dome over whatever was burning. But the smoke wasn't moving. It just sat there like some sort of giant cloudy planet had floated down to earth and sunk halfway into the ground.

"There it is," Irk said as he stopped, took another

deep drink of dark, and shook his head ominously at the Good Times Ravine.

"It doesn't look like a good time to me," Karen said, stopping to look at the thick dome of smoke.

As Karen was taking in the scenery, I looked over and saw something very strange.

"What are those?" I asked as I pointed toward what looked like a bunch of giant water balloons rolling slowly across the horizon.

"Just Blevins," Irk said like I should already have known what they were.

"Blevins?" I asked, confused. "Are they alive?"

"Of course they're alive," he said impatiently. "They're *Blevins*."

"You keep saying it like I'm supposed to know what they are," I said, just as impatiently. "I'm not from here, remember? Are they friendly?"

"They're nothing," he said with a sigh that was supposed to tell me what a pain I was being. "They just roll around all day and night and soak the nutrients out of the ground. They're just big pests, if you ask me."

"Does anybody eat them?" Karen asked.

"None of *us* do," Irk said, like Karen's question was normal even though if I had asked it I'm sure he would have made it seem like I was the biggest dope ever. "But they sure love them down in the ravine."

"Wait a minute," I said nervously, my stomach suddenly dropping several inches toward my feet. "*Who* loves them in the ravine? Is there something that eats things inside all that smoke?"

"Of course there is," Irk said in his impatient now-I'm-talking-to-the-goofball-Iggy-instead-of-the-smart-and-pretty-Karen tone. "Why do you think I said the Good Times Ravine was dangerous? 'Cause you'll get hurt having too much fun?"

"Dangerous is one thing but getting eaten is a whole other thing. I mean, if something eats you, it usually eats you alive, right? And then you're all dead and chewed up and going through whatever-ate-you's digestive tract and then he poops you out and you're just this big turd that nobody knows used to be a person with hopes and dreams and then they—"

"All right, Iggy, *enough*!" Karen said, holding up one hand in front of my face. "Can you have your breakdown some other time? You're grossing me out."

Completely freaked, I looked around for something to distract me so that I could get my mind off my possible future as a pile of doody. And that was when I saw something shiny on the ground.

"I wouldn't worry about it," Irk said to Karen. "Blevins are so stupid anything can catch them. They fall for the dumbest traps."

I walked toward the shiny thing and saw it was some kind of silver mushroom that was sticking up out of the mud.

"Blevins are attracted to anything that's bright," I heard Irk saying behind me as I bent down to look at the shiny little toadstool. "They think any shiny thing is the sun. Even if it's on the ground sticking up out of the mud."

"You mean something like this?" I asked as Irk and Karen turned to see the silver mushroom I was pointing at.

"Iggy!" Irk yelled as his eye went wide. "Get away from that!"

"But I—"

That's about all I got out because the mud under my feet exploded up into the air and what looked like a big round blanket that I was standing in the middle of flew up and closed around me like a cocoon.

"Oh, no…" was all I heard Karen say as her face filled with panic.

The blanket then cinched tight around my neck

so that only my head was sticking out as I said, "Can somebody get me out of—"

I couldn't finish *that* sentence because suddenly my feet were yanked out from under me and my cocoon was pulled through the mud away from Karen and Irk at about a million miles an hour as I was reeled in fast like a fish on a line.

"Iggy!" I heard Karen yell as she quickly disappeared into the distance.

It felt like I was being dragged behind a speedboat by my legs. My body was protected from the ground

by the cocoon, except for the fact that a ton of mud was going up my nose since my head was still sticking out.

I saw Irk bouncing after me with Karen clinging to his back. But I was going so fast it was clear that they would never catch up. If I was going to get out of this mess, I was going to have to get out of it myself.

I tried to move my hands up to pull the cinched blanket away from my neck, but they were clamped against my sides. I attempted to slide them up and over my stomach but tiny bristles that moved like little fingers grabbed my skin and held my arms in place. This wasn't a blanket at all. This thing was alive!

Starting to panic, I tried to kick my legs but more bristles grabbed onto me and locked me in place. I couldn't do anything except continue to get mud packed up my nose as whatever it was that had me kept on pulling me toward whatever dinner table I was about to be the main course on.

Totally freaked, I realized I had to do *something* to save myself. And so I blasted a huge fart.

I mean, hey, since this thing was alive and since I knew that the berry fart I had inside me would probably be pretty deadly, I let loose with what I was sure would be my stinkiest cheese-cutting to date. My gaseous expulsion was so loud and powerful that the whole cocoon vibrated from the blast. I know that if I was holding onto someone and they ripped a foghorn like the one I just did, I wouldn't be able to let go of them fast enough.

I immediately felt all the bristles around me go limp and was able to flip myself over, getting my nose out of the mud so that now the back of my head was dragging through the sludge. But then as soon as I tried to pull my arms up, the bristles went stiff and grabbed onto me again. Sadly, the fart hadn't done much except encase me in the vilest-smelling odor ever to come out of my body. So not only was I being dragged toward my death but I also felt like I was about to throw up.

I needed a plan B.

I thought for a second and then decided to use the only thing available to me.

My teeth.

I bent my head forward and chomped down on the cinched up cocoon collar around my neck. I was so desperate that I bit right through it, a big chunk coming off in my mouth.

The cocoon flinched and loosened its grip around my neck. I quickly pulled my arms free. But the pain of my bite made whatever was pulling me start reeling me in even faster. The spraying mud was hitting me like needles being shot out of a cannon and I could see we were almost at the big purple-and-yellow dome of smoke that covered the ravine. I struggled to free myself but the cocoon was still gripping my legs and waist too tightly.

I was in big trouble.

And that was when I felt something wrap around my chest like a rope.

I looked up and saw Swiff staring me right in the face.

"I *knew* you'd need me!" she said happily, completely unfazed by the fact that we were being dragged through the mud faster than a race car.

"Swiff, get me out of here," I said, extremely pleased to see her.

"Anything you want, boyfriend!"

And with that, she wrapped her leaves around my chest, spread her roots out like a pitchfork, and stuck them deep into the mud.

POP!

Before I knew what was happening, my body was yanked out of the cocoon, the bristles no match for Swiff's sudden stop. It felt like my ribs had been crushed by a pair of pliers from her grip but one thing was for certain: I wasn't in the cocoon anymore.

Swiff groaned a little, showing that the sudden stop had hurt her also, but she quickly recovered and turned to look at me.

"How was that, boyfriend?" she asked with a giggle.

"That was fantastic!" I said, feeling like I wanted to cry with joy.

We both smiled at each other, and then I looked to see where we were.

And that was when I realized we weren't out of trouble yet.

21
Good Times

We were in the ravine.

And, I have to say, it certainly did look like good times.

We were at the top of an incline that slowly sloped down to what looked like a forest made out of marshmallows or something. I know that sounds kind of dumb, but it *did* sort of look like that. It wasn't until I looked closer that I saw that the marshmallowy things were actually big, weird-looking mushrooms. Tons of them

for as far as I could see. Some were as tall as buildings, and filled in all around those were lots of smaller ones, still as big as houses.

The purple-and-yellow smoke had created a low ceiling over the huge forest, and the whole thing roiled and billowed like we were underwater. The glow from the colorful clouds overhead lit up and tinted the ground so that the whole place looked like something out of a comic book. But the most realistic-looking comic book ever.

"Well, this is strange," I said as Swiff and I stared at the sight in front of us. "Have you ever been here before?"

"No, only Irk has seen it and lived," Swiff said matter-of-factly. "He wouldn't tell us about it because he said it was such a bad place. But it doesn't look bad to me."

"Yeah, it doesn't look like the terrible place he said it was," I said, staring at the way the clouds reflected colors onto the tops of the mushrooms. It made them look almost like big dirty cupcakes. "Although something in that forest just tried to kill me."

"Maybe it just liked you and wanted you to come visit its home," she said as she moved up next to me and fluttered her eye. "I know I would."

I don't know what it was about me and girls from other frequencies. Girls back home avoided me like I was a wheelbarrow filled with dead mice but for some reason I seemed to be quite a hunk in places with alternative evolution. And I was sort of desperate to know why.

"Why do you like me so much, Swiff?"

She stared at me for a few seconds, like she couldn't figure out the question. Then she finally said...

"Because you're famous."

"That's it?" I asked, thrown by her answer.

"Why? Isn't that enough?"

"Not really," I said, feeling a little disappointed. "Not if that's the only reason you like me."

"I also like you because you're the Meat Master of Games," she said brightly, like she was sure this would be a better answer.

"But that's why I'm 'famous.'"

"No, you're famous because you're from another world. And now you're my boyfriend!"

All of Swiff's talk about boyfriends and girlfriends suddenly made me think of...

"Iggy!" a girl's voice yelled.

I looked up and saw Foo! She was the flying girl

from the last frequency who actually *did* like me and she was hovering over the mushroom forest! She was far away but I knew it was her.

"Foo!" I called out in shock. "What are you doing here?"

"I came to get you," she said back. She was speaking quietly and yet for some reason I could hear her like she was standing next to me.

"I can't believe you're here!" I called as I started walking down the incline in her direction.

"I figured out the transporter," she said as I began to run down the muddy incline, my feet slipping as I picked up speed.

"Iggy!" I heard Swiff call after me. "Where are you going?"

But I just kept running toward Foo.

"After the fire, we all dug out the transporter," Foo said as she came down lower and hovered right above the tall mushrooms at the edge of the forest, "Peepup, Feep Feep, and I figured out how to use it. I came back to get you. We all did."

I looked and saw Peepup and Feep Feep standing just inside the forest, waving at me. And then my first friend from that other frequency, the cat that thought it was a dog, popped out and started spinning in circles like it couldn't believe it was seeing me.

"C'mon, Iggy!" Peepup called. "You've gotta see the transporter! We know how to use it."

As they waved for me to follow and then took off into the forest, I sprinted even faster, mud flying up behind me.

"Iggy! Stop!"

I looked over my shoulder and saw Karen and Irk running down the incline toward where Swiff was standing and staring at me.

"Karen, it's Foo!" I yelled back as I kept running. "They know how to get us out of here!"

"But, Iggy! She's not—!"

Before Karen could finish I ran past the first mushroom tree and into the forest. Peepup and Feep Feep and the cat were running ahead of me, waving their arms and telling me to follow them.

"It's this way, Iggy," Feep Feep called back to me. I'd never seen him run this fast before and was sort of surprised he *could* even run, being that he was a stumpy mole and all.

"Through here," Foo called down from above me as she pointed to a gap that ran through the dense wall of mushrooms. There were so many mushrooms of different shapes and sizes growing close together that I started to wonder if I was going to be able to get much farther into this place.

I ran through the gap and into total darkness. Suddenly afraid that I might run face-first into some mushroom trunk, I stopped.

"Foo?" I called out. "Guys? Where is everybody?"

"Just keep walking forward," Foo's voice said. "You're almost there."

I stumbled forward through the dark, my hands out in front of me. Maybe this wasn't such a good idea, I thought. But Foo was here. What could be better than that?

My hand hit something that felt like a wall of soft ropes. I pushed my hands into it, pulled open a space, and walked through it.

Bright light hit my eyes and I had to snap them shut and put my hands up to my face to shield myself. I felt warmth on my skin and realized I was feeling something I hadn't felt in a few days...

Sunlight.

I squinted and saw something that I couldn't believe.

My home.

I was back in front of my house in the neighborhood

I grew up in. My parents were standing at the front door and Foo was hovering next to them.

"Mom? Dad?" I said in almost a whisper, since I couldn't believe what I was seeing. "Foo, how did you do this?"

"I told you we figured out how to use the transporter," she said with a smile.

My mom and dad ran over and hugged me so tightly I couldn't breathe.

And I didn't care.

I was home.

"We have no idea what's going on or where you've been but we're so happy you're back," my mom said as tears rolled down her cheeks.

"And I know you're probably upset about losing my Shakespeare book," my dad said, pretending to be mad but then breaking into a huge smile. "I can get another one. But I can never get another Ignatius."

And then he hugged me and my mom hugged me again and then Foo hugged me and the cat who thought it was a dog jumped into my arms and it was the best thing I could ever have imagined happening to me ever. I was home, Foo was here, and all was right with the world.

"Why don't you have a lie down?" my mom said as

she gestured over to the super comfortable lawn chair that my dad always spent every weekend in.

"Be my guest," said my dad as he patted me on the back.

I smiled at him, and stepped over to the chair and was just about to sit down on it when...

22
Slap!!!

Something hit me hard across my face. I spun sideways, and when I opened my eyes, I was standing in the middle of a small clearing surrounded by mushroom trees.

No parents, no lawn chair, no bright sunlight, and no Foo.

All I saw was Karen standing there, her arm cocked back, ready to hit me once more.

"Iggy, wake up!" she yelled as she slapped me again, this time even harder.

"OW!" I screamed. My face felt like it was on fire. "Quit hitting me!"

"You were hallucinating," she said apologetically. "That's how they eat you here."

"Huh?" I said as the happiness of having been back home with my family and Foo was replaced by the now familiar fear of being eaten.

"This air is filled with Good Times gas," said Irk. "It's used to trigger happy thoughts in your brain and makes you think you see whatever relaxes you the most. Once you lie down, your body soaks up their poison and you die and then they eat you."

"*Who* eats you?" I asked, feeling sort of sick to my stomach that I had almost taken a deadly lie down in my dad's lawn chair.

"*They* do," Irk said, gesturing at the mushroom trees all around us.

I looked down and saw that every inch of the ground, including right under our feet, was covered with tiny mushrooms.

"Ew, can they kill us through our feet?" I asked as I started bouncing around to avoid standing on the killer mushrooms.

"Not easily, but they can if we stand here long enough," Irk said as I saw Karen secretly start shifting her feet around too. "Which is why we should keep moving. But we have to keep an eye on each other. If we notice any one of us starting to act strangely, we have to slap that person right away."

Karen glanced over at me with a look that said "You better be sure I'm really in trouble before you slap me." Then she looked at Swiff, whose expression showed she couldn't wait to land a hard one across Karen's face.

Karen glared at her, then turned to Irk. "Lead the way," she said.

And off into the dense mushroom forest we went.

A plate of French fries.

Then another plate of French fries.

Then a bottle of ketchup.

They floated around my head, then drifted over to a big soft bed with a TV at the foot of it.

All my favorite shows were on.

"Oh, man, that looks so great," I said as I stared at the wonderful scene before me.

SLAP!!!

Karen practically knocked my teeth out.

"Cut it out!" I yelled. "I *know* it's not real!"

"I can't take a chance," she said innocently. "I have to protect you."

"You just like hitting me, don't you?"

"Of course not, Iggy. It hurts me more than it hurts you," she said with a smile.

"I seriously doubt that," I said as I rubbed my now raw cheek.

"Iggy!" we heard Swiff yell, "You really do like me! Yes, I'll sit on the ground with you!"

Swiff started toward a tall mushroom tree but Irk grabbed her and slapped her across the petals.

"Stay with us, Swiff," Irk said as he shook her stem.

"I was just talking to Iggy," she said angrily.

"No, you weren't."

"Yes, I was! He's standing right there," she said, pointing over at me.

"That's not the Iggy you were talking to because he didn't really say anything to you."

"Yes, he did, didn't you, Iggy?"

"Uh, no," I said, feeling sort of bad for her.

"C'mon, daisy," Karen grumbled. "Can't you get the hang of this whole hallucination thing?"

"You're just jealous because he likes me more than you!" Swiff yelled as she tried to break free of Irk's grip to attack Karen.

"You're nuts," Karen said, stepping forward. "And if you want to fight me, then bring it on. Nothing would make me happier."

Swiff tried to lunge again but Irk had too strong a grip on her.

Karen charged forward and suddenly ran right past Irk and Swiff.

"All right, weed, it's *go time*!" Karen yelled as she ran off into the forest. "Not so tough without Irk holding you back now, huh? Come back here and stop running!"

Irk and I looked at each other.

"Where's she going?" asked Swiff.

"Uh-oh..." said Irk and then we all took off after Karen, who was way ahead of us, darting in and out of mushroom trunks, grabbing at a fleeing Swiff who wasn't really there.

"C'mon, flower girl!" she taunted as she ran. "Let's settle this once and for all!"

"Karen!" I yelled as we dodged through the forest. "She's not really ahead of you! She's back here with us. You're just seeing things!"

Karen spun to look at me and suddenly fell backward and disappeared with a short scream.

"KAREN!" I yelled.

Irk and I sprinted forward and stopped suddenly.

We were at the peak of a hill. We saw Karen tumbling down toward a second valley that was covered with big round mushroom caps that looked almost like the throw pillows my grandma had all over her house.

"Karen!" I called after her. "Don't lie down when you get to the bottom!"

"I don't think I'll ever *get* to the bottom!" she yelled as she banged down the hill like an out-of-control crash test dummy.

Irk scooped me up under his frond and started hopping down the hill after Karen. I could see that the mushroom trees at the bottom of this valley were much taller than the ones we just ran through, as Karen went tumbling through an opening in the trees and disappeared from view.

"Hurry, Irk!" I yelled, suddenly scared that something really bad might happen to Karen. Whether I wanted to admit it or not, I really cared about her, and the thought of being trapped in any frequency without her was more than I could stand.

Irk took a huge flying leap and landed right in the gap Karen had gone through.

I jumped from his frond and we all ran in, unsure what to expect.

"Oh, *gross*!" I heard Karen yell as we came through

an archway of mushrooms and found ourselves inside what looked like an enormous igloo the size of an indoor football stadium. Its domed roof was made out of long thin mushrooms that had woven themselves into a basket pattern and the ground was covered with small slimy toadstools. It was really hot and humid and felt like what I imagine the inside of someone's stomach would be like.

I scanned around but couldn't see Karen. However, I did notice that there were dead Blevins lying all over the place. Out of a big hole in the center of the ground, several leathery-looking vines stretched like tightropes extended out through various openings in the dome's walls.

All of a sudden, one of the vines began to reel in quickly. *POONK!* A cocoon holding a Blevin popped through a hole and came flying toward us. The Blevin sailed through the air, then landed heavily on the ground with a fat wet thump and rolled like a gooey bowling ball. It slowed to a stop and then deflated a bit, like it just gave its final breath.

"Can somebody get me out of here?" Karen called from some unknown place.

"Where are you?" yelled Irk. "Can you move?"

"I'm stuck," said Karen. "Uch, this is disgusting."

We looked in the direction of her voice, but the

only thing I could see was another big Blevin lying in the mushrooms up ahead. It was larger than the other Blevins and almost looked like it was vibrating. Just then, Karen's arm popped up out of some deep mushrooms a few feet in front of it.

We all ran over, and Irk and I grabbed her arm and tried to pull her up. She was covered with slippery, super gross black goo that stank like the world's dirtiest pair of underwear, which made it hard to get a grip on her.

"Don't fall asleep!" Irk yelled down at her.

"Don't worry," she called back. "I'm too busy trying not to barf."

Seeing how much trouble we were having, Swiff ran up, wrapped her stem tightly around Karen's wrist, and pulled hard.

SHLORK!

Karen popped up out of what must have been a huge sinkhole of goop. She was covered from head to toe with the stuff. She spit out a huge mouthful and then screamed like she was losing her mind.

"GAAAHHH!!! That's so GROSS!!!"

As she continued to spit more of the black stuff out, I heard a noise. I looked over at the Blevin next to us, which was making deep rumbling sounds as it continued to vibrate.

"Is it alive?" I asked as I stepped over to it.

"No, it's extremely dead," said Irk as he tried to brush more of the goop off Karen's arms.

"Iggy, get away from that thing," Karen said as she wiped black sludge out of her eyes. "I've seen enough gross stuff for one day."

"Hey, it couldn't be any grosser than what just happened to you," I said as I reached out to feel the Blevin's skin. I know I should have been grossed out by something dead but it just sort of looked like a big beach ball.

"No, don't touch it!" Irk yelled about a nanosecond after my fingers touched the Blevin's skin.

BLAM!

The Blevin exploded like a giant popped balloon, blowing tons of super smelly dark green guts everywhere.

"Well, I was wrong," Karen said with a sigh as the Blevin innards continued to rain down on us. "I guess I *hadn't* seen enough gross things today."

Yeah, but now I officially had.

23

Almost There

Man, did we stink.

We'd done our best to wipe off the Blevin guts that had covered every part of our bodies, but without any pools of water or towels or soap there was nothing we could really do except scrape off the excess and try not to think about it.

As we continued our journey through the ravine, I kept seeing bathtubs and swimming pools and showers. But by this point I had learned enough about how the Good Times gas worked to realize that anything I saw that was too good to be true was just that.

Swiff would occasionally run and jump into some invisible pond, but Irk had gotten good at grabbing her quickly and slapping her back to reality. Once even Karen thought we were approaching a big lake and dove into a pile of bright yellow toadstools. I ran and grabbed her, but by the time I had gotten my courage up to slap her, she snapped out of her hallucination and said, "Your hand touches my cheek and it'll be the last thing you ever touch in this life."

As we made our way across an open field of mushrooms that Irk called the Happy Flats (aptly named since all my eyes kept seeing as we walked were floating candy bars, cans of soda, plates of spaghetti, pieces of pizza, and hot dogs on a stick swirling through the

air), Karen shook her head hard and slapped her own cheek.

"Man, that gas really gets inside your brain," she said as she tried to refocus her eyes. "Irk, don't you ever see things because of it?"

"Not really," he said with a shrug. "Trees don't get affected by it. Not like the plants and Blevins do."

He looked over at Swiff, who was staring up in the air and grabbing at unseen things with her leaves, saying, "Look at all the cups of dark!"

"Are you immune to the gas?" Karen asked as Irk reached out and gently tapped Swiff's petals, bringing her back to earth.

"No, we're just too smart to fall for it," he said matter-of-factly. Karen looked insulted.

"If you do say so yourself."

"Hey, no offense," said Irk. "The trees have always known about the ravine and they use the actual gas to train us when we're young so we won't be affected by it."

"How do they do that?" Karen asked as I saw her shake her head again, trying hard not to give in to some vision she was starting to see.

"They fill our room with the gas and we see wonderful things we wish existed and then they walk around and slap us. Then they pump in more gas and we see more great things and they slap us and they pump in more gas and slap us and slap us and slap us for weeks and months until our brains refuse to even bother showing us something wonderful that's not there. That's why the few times in our lives that we do see good things, we know they're actually real. The problem is we never see anything good. Not back in the tree city."

Irk stopped and grabbed his side in pain again. But this time he doubled over like he was really hurting.

Karen walked over and put her hand on his back.

"Are you all right?"

"Yeah, I guess," he said, still bent over. "I just really need some dark."

Irk raised his head and looked at something he thought he saw above him. He held his fronds up toward the sky. Then he angrily shook his head and slapped himself across the face. I winced when he did it because he whacked himself so hard that he almost fell over.

"What did you see?" I asked cautiously.

"Nothing," he said, embarrassed.

"You need sunlight, don't you?" Karen asked. "More than you need dark. I saw it in the tree city. There's always sunlight. That's how you survive."

Irk looked at Karen and stared for a moment. Then he looked over at Swiff, who was preoccupied with some imaginary dark-sipping party she was having with a bunch of her invisible friends.

"Have you ever been to California?" Irk asked quietly.

Karen and I looked at each other, surprised.

"What do you know about California?" she asked in disbelief.

"I know that it's always sunny and there are lots of trees like me but they can't walk or fight and if I went there I'd be famous and have everything I've ever wanted."

Needless to say, we were both a little thrown by Irk's sudden knowledge of something from our frequency which, up until this moment, he had seemed to know nothing about.

"Who told you all that?" I asked.

He looked again to make sure Swiff wasn't listening and then said in a whisper...

"Herbert."

Karen sat back on her heels and studied Irk for a few seconds.

"Why would he tell you about California when he didn't even tell you about the transporter?"

193

Irk looked thrown for the first time since I'd met him. He creaked out an "Umm," then quickly regrouped.

"He mentioned it to me when we were carrying the gold through here. He said it was a place someone else had told him about. He wasn't sure if it was real or not. He just thought I'd be interested in it because of the kind of tree I am. He called me a *palm tree*."

Karen stared at him for a long time, like she was trying to figure everything out.

"California is back in our frequency," she said, confused. "I don't understand why he'd tell you about it if he didn't tell you about the transporter and all the other frequencies he'd been to. It doesn't make sense."

"Hey, the guy stole all our gold!" Irk snapped angrily, surprising Karen. "I don't know why he does what he does. I asked because I thought maybe Herbert told you about it, too. I just wondered if you knew how to get to this California place because I'd like to go there before I die from lack of sunlight, okay?"

"Well, we're not going anywhere if you just stand there and don't show us where this stupid cave is," Karen snapped back at him. "You don't think we're hungry and feel cruddy, too?"

"Fine," Irk said, testy. "Let's just go, okay?"

"Fine with me," Karen said as she turned and looked

at Swiff, who was laughing at some unheard joke her fantasy friends had just told.

As Irk stormed off, still holding his side painfully, Karen slapped Swiff, said, "C'mon, Alice in Wonderland," and then stomped off after Irk.

Well, at least she wasn't mad at *me* for once.

24
Fun in the Forest

There was nothing beautiful about the Life is Beautiful Forest.

This is because the Life is Beautiful Forest was a forest of rocks. Big, tall rock pillars that went way up high into the air. It was set down in the lowest part of the ravine and the walls that surrounded it had several openings up high that black goop was pouring out of. Which meant that the floor of the forest was covered with several inches of the stinky stuff.

"This is really disgusting," Karen said, then almost slipped and fell as we made our way cautiously through the black glop. "Isn't this stuff the same as dark? Can't you just drink it to make yourself feel better?"

Irk gave Karen a sarcastic look and said, "Blevins look like big berries. Can't you just eat *them* to make yourself feel better?"

"I'm just trying to help." She sighed.

"This is fungus food," he said, pointing at the gooey black on the ground. "And I'm not a fungus."

"Geez," Karen said under her breath. "Touchy."

I'd heard my mom call my dad *touchy* before, so it wasn't like I'd never heard the word. But for some reason when Karen said it, it struck me as really funny. So funny, in fact, that I started to laugh.

"What's your problem?" Karen asked, looking at me like I was nuts.

"I don't know," I said as I began to laugh harder. "You said 'touchy.'"

"Yeah, *and*? Touchy's not funny."

"For some reason, it is," I said as I really started to crack up. "It's really, really funny."

And with that, I doubled over with laughter. Swiff

burst out laughing, too, and her laugh started to make me laugh even harder. Soon, the two of us were laughing so hard we could barely breathe.

"Stop laughing, you idiots!" Karen yelled. But as soon as she did, a smile came over her face and she started to giggle. "None of this is funny."

I guess trying not to laugh only made her want to laugh more, like when you're sitting in church and somebody's stomach growls during a really quiet moment and you know you'll get in major trouble if you even so much as snicker.

The next thing we knew, Karen, Swiff, and I were practically helpless with laughter.

"Why am I laughing?" Karen wheezed.

"It's the gas in here," Irk said as he kept walking forward. "They're trying to make you laugh so hard you'll pass out."

"It makes perfect sense," Karen said as she doubled over with laughter. "But I know how to stop it."

She stumbled over to me and cocked her arm back. Irk looked over and saw her just as she started to swing her hand toward my face.

"Wait, Karen. That won't—"

SLAP!!!

She practically knocked my head off as I fell against a rock pillar, my face stinging like somebody had just pressed a hot iron against it. My eyes welled up like I was going to start crying and then...

I started to laugh even harder.

"That only makes it worse," Irk said as he headed over to us.

"*Now* you tell her," I said as my knees went out from under me and I fell onto my butt in the disgusting black mushroom food. I was laughing harder than the time I saw Ivan accidentally sneeze into a glass of milk he was drinking, which made it spray like a fire hose into his face.

As we all cracked up even more, Irk came over and grabbed Karen by the shoulders.

"You all have to stop laughing!" he yelled. "If you pass out, we can't get to the transporter."

"I know," she said, screaming with laughter. "How do we stop? Think of something sad, right?"

"No, that'll make you laugh even harder," he said urgently.

"Then what do we do?!" she sputtered in hysterics.

"You have to—"

Irk stopped. His eyes went wide as he stared at something behind Karen. Then...

"RUN FOR YOUR LIVES!"

We all turned and our jaws dropped. Because standing behind us was a huge Tyrannosaurus rex. It bent down and roared in our faces, its razor sharp teeth inches from my nose.

We all screamed and took off running as fast as we could through the ooze-covered rock forest. I looked over my shoulder and saw that the T. rex was running after us, snapping its teeth as it maneuvered through the tall pillars like an Olympic skier on a downhill run.

"He's gaining on us!" I yelled as we darted in and out of the tall rocks, our feet slipping under us. "We have to hide somewhere!"

"There's nowhere *to* hide!" Karen shouted, her eyes darting around wildly.

"The cave is up ahead!" Irk shouted as he jumped over a rock pillar that had fallen down many years ago.

"Where did a dinosaur come from?" I shouted to Karen as the T. rex lunged, almost biting my butt off.

"It's not a dinosaur, you idiot!" Karen yelled. "It's some kind of giant mutant Blevin!"

"No, it's not," I called back. "It's a T. rex!"

"What are you guys, blind?" Swiff called over. "It's one of the tree army's killing machines!"

Karen and I looked at each other, then over at Irk, who made a face. We slowed down our run, then turned and looked behind us.

The T. rex was still running full speed, roaring and ready to pounce. I looked at Karen, she looked at me, and then we both slapped each other hard across the cheek at the exact same moment.

Everything went silent as the T. rex disappeared. The only sound was our double face slap echoing through the stone forest.

Karen turned and looked at Irk.

"There wasn't anything chasing us, was there?"

"Hey, you wanted to stop laughing," he said. "Fear's the only thing that stops it."

"Oh, man," she said as she put her face in her hands. "A giant Blevin. How embarrassing. It's like being afraid of a cow."

"A what?" Swiff asked.

"Never mind," said Karen. "How long 'til we get to the cave?"

"Turn around," Irk said as he pointed past us.

We looked and saw a long rocky incline coming up

out of the black goop. At the top of it was the opening of a large, dark cave.

"Welcome to the Cave of Smiles," Irk said ominously.

Yeah, welcome indeed.

25
That Cave I Was
Just Talking About

As we walked up the incline to the cave, all I could
hear were our footsteps crunching in the gravel under
our feet and the goopy-sounding drips of black ooze
coming out of the walls behind us. I looked over at
Irk and saw that his eye was filled with fear. Swiff,
however, was bouncing along as usual, oblivious to any
possible danger we might be approaching.

"Slow down, Swiff," Irk said when she started to

move ahead of him. "I don't think you and I should get much closer."

"Is this the place with the curse?" she asked as happily as a person might ask the ice cream man what flavors he had.

Irk stopped walking and touched his chest.

"I'm starting to feel the tingle," he said, dread in his voice. "We have to wait at the bottom, Swiff."

"But I want to go with them," she pleaded. "They'll need my help. I don't care about any curse."

"Irk's right, Swiff," Karen said. "We can't take any chances if there's something here that's going to hurt you. Let Iggy and me do this. We know what we're looking for."

"Do you feel anything?" Irk asked Karen and me. "Any tingling? Tightness?"

We looked at each other. I felt fine, other than the fact that I was covered with dried black ooze that smelled like the feet of someone who hadn't taken a bath in a year.

"We're good so far," said Karen. Then she sniffed the air, noticing something. "But something's weird. Like some sort of chemical. Do you smell that, Iggy?"

I sniffed and despite all the stinkiness around

me, Karen was right. There was the smallest trace of something.

"It almost smells like bug spray," I said, confused.

"You two should head back down," Karen said to Irk and Swiff. "Whatever it is, I bet it's coming from the cave, and it's probably what made Irk sick the last time."

Irk gave Karen a nod, then grabbed one of Swiff's leaves and started to pull her down the incline.

"No, please! Let me go with them!" she begged like a little kid being dragged out of a carnival. "I wanna help!"

But Irk just kept walking as he looked back over his shoulder and said, "If the transporter is there, let me know. Don't leave without telling me."

Karen turned to me and took a deep breath. "Okay, Ig, you ready to check out the Cave of Smiles?"

I forced a big goofy grin at her, trying to be funny, but neither one of us was in much of a comedy-enjoying mood.

"Yeah, let's do it," I said as we continued walking toward the cave.

The chemical smell definitely started to get stronger the closer we got. I looked and saw that there were piles of dead and dried-out plants and vines around the mouth of the cave. Some, which I guess were the fighters who had been ambushed by Herbert's army, looked like they had been all chopped up. But other plants seemed like they had just fallen down dead in their tracks. These must have been some of the plants that Irk said had tried to come and visit the cave. I could only imagine how many others hadn't even made it this far and were just part of the black sludge.

Karen started coughing.

"Are you okay?" I asked about a second before I also started to cough. The chemical smell was getting stronger. "Do you think it's poisoning us, too?"

"I don't think so," Karen said as she picked up the tail of her shirt and tried to brush the dried black crust off it. "But let's cover our faces just to be sure. Whatever it is, it can't be good for us."

I pulled the collar of my T-shirt up over my mouth and nose so that I looked a bit like a bank robber in an old cowboy movie.

"What's that sound?" Karen asked as we got to the mouth of the cave.

I strained to hear and noticed a quiet hissing sound coming from inside the cave. "You don't think it's like some poisonous snake or anything...do you?"

"I don't know," Karen said as she slowly got into her

kung fu stance and went ahead of me. "But this sure is a bad time not to have a sword."

Sssssssssssssssssssssssssss. The sound and smell got stronger as we stepped into the cave. It didn't sound like an animal, though. It sounded like something was leaking.

"Mystery solved," Karen said over her shoulder. I walked up next to her and saw two big metal canisters sitting inside recesses on both sides of the cave. A label on the side of one read ORTHO WEED AND PLANT KILLER. The other said ROUNDUP TREE BE GONE HERBICIDE.

Karen walked over to the tree-killing canister and turned a knob on the top of it. The hissing stopped. I turned off the weed killer and the cave went silent.

"Should we tell Irk and Swiff?" I asked.

"It's gonna take a while for this to clear since there's no breeze," she said as she peered into the dark cave. "Let's just keep going. We know what we're looking for. I just hope it's in here."

I hoped so, too. I also hoped there wasn't anything *else* in here, if you know what I mean.

26
Good News and Bad News

Man, were we underprepared for cave exploration.

First of all, when you go into a dark cave, it's very helpful if you have a flashlight. Or a torch. Or a match. Or anything that lights up. Because, you know, caves are kind of famous for being dark since they're tunnels that don't have any windows.

Second of all, you should have some kind of protection. I mean, kung fu is all well and good but chances are that if something attacks you in the dark, you'll be inside its stomach before you can throw your first karate chop.

Well, we didn't have a light *or* protection, so while we were slowly being swallowed up by the darkness as we walked deeper and deeper into the cave, I felt like I might as well just sprinkle salt and pepper on my head and ring the dinner bell.

"I *really* do not have a good feeling about this," I said as my hands felt their way along the cave wall.

"Don't be such a baby," Karen said from the other side. "You don't always need to use your eyes. Listen for things. Use your sense of touch."

"How can I not?" I said, trying to hold it together. "*I can't see!*"

"Look, with all that tree and plant killer, nothing from this frequency would be alive in here anyway."

"Yeah, but what about something *not* from this frequency?"

Karen was silent for a few seconds. Then she said, "Just shut up and keep moving, would you?"

I stepped forward and bashed my foot into a rock.

"OW!"

"What's the matter?!" Karen called, startled.

"I stubbed my toe."

"Could you please hold all shouts for actual emergencies?" she said, testy.

"I'm sorry. It's only the toe on the foot that I have to walk on in order to *survive*."

"Have you ever been nominated for an Oscar for best dramatic performance by an actress? 'Cause I think you'd win—OW!"

"What happened?!" I called out, freaked.

"I stubbed my—never mind."

"Man, you're such a hypocri—"

My foot slipped out from under me as I stepped on something hard and smooth. And the next thing I knew I was sliding on my butt down what felt and sounded like a metal ramp.

A *long* metal ramp.

"Iggy!" I heard Karen call out as I zoomed down the ramp like I was on one of those tall metal slides they have at amusement parks. For some reason my butt used to get stuck on those and I'd always stop halfway. But not on this slide, which I was now flying down at an alarming speed.

"Karen!" I yelled. "I can't stop!"

"I'm coming, Iggy!" she yelled as I heard her jump onto the ramp.

The ramp turned a corner, which made me crash into the wall and start tumbling head over heels, out of control. But as I was rolling and smacking my face on the metal and scraping my arms on the rocky walls, I saw light reflecting off the ramp up ahead. And then, all of a sudden, the ramp ended and I went flying into a big, dimly lit room, smashing down onto the dirt floor and kicking up a cloud of dust.

"Ow!" I heard Karen yell as she hit the bend in the ramp and probably smacked her face on the wall like I had seconds earlier.

"End of the line coming!" I yelled. "Get ready for a hard landi—"

SMASH! Karen flew off the ramp and knocked into me full force as dirt flew everywhere.

"Oh, man, that wasn't fun," Karen said as we both coughed and choked on all the dust that was floating around us and glowing from the light in the room.

We waved our hands to clear the air and were suddenly able to make out exactly where we were.

We were lying on the ground in front of a huge frequency transporter.

It was humming quietly and small lights all over it were glowing. The computer screen that controlled it was lit up but blank.

"I've never been happier to see anything in my life," Karen said, a big relieved smile on her face.

I noticed something shiny on the ground under the transporter. At first I was worried it was another one of those metal mushrooms that the ravine used to lure Blevins (and Ignatius MacFarlands) into cocoon traps. But when I looked closer I saw that it was yellow.

It was a piece of gold.

Karen saw what I was staring at and stood up. "Looks like Herbert dropped one."

She walked over and picked up the gold as I went over to the computer screen.

"Careful, Iggy," she said. "Don't mess with the transporter until we can figure it out more. If it disappears now, we're really screwed."

"Yeah, I'm sort of used to us being screwed," I said as I stared at the blank screen. "I just want to see if we can turn it on. It looks like it's asleep."

"Let me do it," she said, bumping me out of the way. "If someone's gonna ruin anything, it's gonna be me. Because if it's you, I'll never forgive you."

"Well, if you mess it up I'll never forgive *you*."

"Yeah, but you *have* to forgive me because I'm the one who protects you."

I wanted to respond but quickly realized that she was right. And so I just kept my mouth shut.

Karen handed me the piece of gold and began to inspect the transporter screen. The gold was a perfectly formed little brick, about one inch long and half an inch wide, and stamped on top of it were little letters that read HG.

"Herbert Golonski," I said.

"Yep," Karen said, preoccupied with the transporter. "He probably stamps his initials on every piece of gold he gets his hands on."

"Yeah, I guess," I said as I put the gold piece in my pocket. "Can't you turn the computer on?"

"I don't know," she said as she tapped the computer screen. "It seems pretty locked up."

"Let me try. I got it to work last time."

"It was a setup last time. We don't know if you did anything or not."

"Then what's the harm in letting me try again?" I asked.

"Last time you touched it we ended up here."

"So? Then if I do the same thing again, then we'll just end up back here anyway, right?"

She stared at me skeptically for a few seconds, then said, "That doesn't make any sense. But be my guest, even though you're not gonna have any better luck than I did."

I stepped up to the screen and moved my fingers over it the same way I had seen Herbert do back in the last frequency when he disappeared with all their gold.

Nothing happened.

I tried again.

Nothing.

"Toldya so," Karen said with a smirk.

"Really?" I said back, suddenly bugged by her. "Are you really gonna say *toldya so*? Aren't you supposed to be more mature than me? Isn't that part of the whole 'girls mature faster than boys' thing?"

"Geez, sorry," she said, rolling her eyes. "Don't get so—"

The transporter beeped.

Karen and I both jumped back, startled.

We stared at the machine. Other than the one beep, nothing was different. The screen was still blank. The lights were still dim.

Thirty seconds passed.

Nothing.

"Maybe it's got like a car alarm in it or something,"

I said, not sure what to think. "Maybe it was telling us to get away from it."

"That's an incredibly dumb theory, Iggy. But maybe we *should* go and tell Irk we found it. We can at least give him back one piece of gold."

I hated the idea of leaving the transporter but since it wasn't working and didn't seem like it was going anywhere, it seemed safe enough to walk away from it for a little while. Maybe Irk would have better luck making it work than we did.

We looked behind us and saw a rocky stairway at the other side of the room that led back up.

"I guess they used the ramp to get the gold down here," Karen said as she headed over to the stairs. "At least these make it easier to get in and out of here. Let's go."

We started to walk up the stairs. As we climbed higher, it seemed like the light wasn't getting dimmer the further away we got from the machine. If anything, it seemed to be getting brighter.

"That's weird," Karen said as she looked down at the stairs. "You didn't find a flashlight, did you?"

"Don't you think I'd tell you if I did?" I said as I turned around to see what was happening.

And that's when I said, "Uh-oh."

The transporter room was getting brighter. Karen and I started back down the stairs and saw that the machine was now glowing so intensely we couldn't even look at it.

"It's gonna disappear!" Karen yelled as the room started to rumble.

"Should we get in it?" I called over the growing noise.

"I can't move toward it!" she yelled as we both started to get pushed back by some invisible force. When the transporter had turned on in the last frequency, we had been able to dive into it. But this time it felt different, like all the energy was coming out of it.

We tried to walk forward but the force was pushing us up the stairs. And then, all of a sudden...

27
Guess Who?

WOOM!

The room exploded with light as Karen and I were thrown backward. We crashed down hard on the stone steps, which knocked the wind out of us.

And then, the bright light was gone.

Karen and I propped ourselves up on our elbows, our eyes practically blinded and our backs aching. We tried to focus our eyes on the transporter.

Oh, man.

Standing under the transporter's arch were six huge creatures that looked like giants. They were ten feet tall, each with two huge arms and two long, thick legs. They didn't have heads, just an indentation between their shoulders with a long slit below it that I guess they could see through. But the weirdest thing about them was that they seemed to be made out of metal.

I don't mean they were robots or guys in suits of armor. They weren't smooth and shiny and sleek. They kind of looked like big piles of metallic rocks, all jagged and bumpy, with sparkles of light reflecting off the shiny speckles that covered them.

The metallic giants didn't have any weapons. They just stood there, slowly scanning the room with their slits. And then we heard the voice.

"Get out of my way."

The metal men in front stepped to the side and Herbert Golonski walked out from between them, still dressed in his suit and tie but now with a translating disc hanging around his neck. He came forward into the room, looked around, and then said, "Now, where's my gold?"

Karen and I were both pressed up against the sides of the stairway, barely able to hide ourselves behind the rocks that jutted out from the walls. There was no way Herbert wasn't going to see us, but if we took off running, we had no idea if the metal guys would be able to catch us or not. And from the scary look of them, I wasn't quite in the mood to find out.

"I know it's in here," said Herbert, glancing back at his metal army. "I can feel it."

I touched the outside of my pocket and felt the outline of the small gold bar inside it. He couldn't be talking about this one little piece of gold, could he? After all the tons of gold he'd already stolen?

I looked over at Karen, who was staring at Herbert's metal men like she was sizing up whether she had any chance if she fought them. And I can tell you that judging by the size of them, no matter how good her kung fu skills were, she didn't.

"They can't have gone far," Herbert said through his translating disc to his small but tall army. "Find them."

The metal guys looked at each other and then started lumbering forward. They looked very slow and stiff as their feet hit heavily down onto the ground. I looked over at Karen and we made a face at each other that said, "Let's get outta here." Without saying a word, Karen and I turned and ran up the stairs.

"There they go," Herbert said. "Get them!"

Suddenly, we heard the metal guys start to run really fast. I glanced over my shoulder and saw what looked like the world's tallest and scariest Olympic running team rocketing up the stairs after us.

"Oh, no, they can run!" I yelled after Karen. "Hyper-speed! Hit hyper-speed!"

She looked back just in time to see two of the metal guys reach out to grab me. I barely ducked under their arms and started sprinting up the stairs so fast that I ran right past her. But then she bolted and flew past me. This girl was fast.

"Through here!" Karen yelled as she got to the top of the stairs and we ducked into an opening that the metal guys wouldn't be able to fit through.

SMASH!

Tons of rock and debris flew past us as the first metal guy ran straight through the wall like he was running through a sheet of Kleenex.

Oh, boy, were we in trouble.

As we ran down the six-foot-tall tunnel, the metal guys simply plowed through it. Rocks were flying everywhere, hitting Karen and me in the back as we shielded our heads with our hands and ran for our lives.

"This is bad," I said to no one in particular. "This is really bad."

"Turn left!" Karen yelled.

We flew around a tight turn and saw that the top of the metal ramp was up ahead. Once we got past that, I knew we were close to the cave's exit. After we got out the exit, though, I had no idea what we were going to do.

Since this part of the cave was tall, the metal guys really picked up speed. The first guy was immediately on our heels and it was clear he was seconds away from grabbing us. I saw the ramp and started to run toward it.

"Iggy! What are you doing?"

"Just keep running!" I yelled as I clamped my hand over the translating disc in case it was able to speak giant metal guy language. "I have an idea."

I ran at the ramp with the metal guy right behind me, then jumped like I was going to slide down it. However, as my right foot hit the slide, I pushed off and leaped left, the rubber sole on my sneaker gripping the metal and giving me traction. The metal guy did the same move. However, his iron foot didn't grip the slippery ramp and his right leg shot out from under him, making him do the splits as his leg went down the slide.

BLAM! He plowed face first into the wall, which exploded into rubble around him.

"Nice work!" Karen yelled as I sprinted up next to her. "Can you get rid of five more?"

BOOM BOOM BOOM!

We heard the footsteps of the other metal guys behind us as the one who hit the wall thrashed around, trying to pull himself out from under the rocks.

"I hope Irk and Swiff can help us," I said as we ran out of the cave and used the downhill slope to pick up speed. Unfortunately, so did our metal pursuers.

"You guys!" Karen yelled as Irk and Swiff turned and saw us. "Got any ideas?"

Their eyes went wide as the five huge metal guys burst out of the cave. Swiff immediately started running toward us as Irk just stood there in shock and watched the approaching army.

"I'll take care of them!" Swiff yelled as she ran at the metal guys, ready for a fight. However, just as she was passing me, I reached out and grabbed her by the middle of her stem, yanked her off her feet, and started carrying her with me.

"I *knew* you loved me!" she yelled happily.

"Just start running *away* from them, Swiff!" I said as I let her go.

"Whatever you say, boyfriend!" she hollered cheerfully as she grabbed my belt loop and started pulling me faster.

Up ahead, Irk was still just standing there, watching all of us approach. I didn't know what he was doing.

"Irk, move!" Karen yelled as we ran past him.

Irk looked back at us, then turned to face the metal men.

"STOP!" he yelled, throwing his frond out in front of him.

Immediately, the metal guys slid to a halt a few feet in front of Irk.

"What's the problem, Herbert?" Irk said as we all stopped and saw Herbert Golonski chugging down the incline after his army. He was sweating and out of breath. With his short legs and round stomach, he was clearly a guy for whom running was not a normal mode of transportation.

"They..." he said, completely winded as he put his hands on his knees and bent over to catch his breath, "...have...my gold."

"You already stole all our gold," Irk said angrily.

"Oh, did I?" Herbert said, still panting but standing up now, trying to sound like he wasn't about to have a heart attack. "I just waltzed in here and overpowered all of you? Stole your gold by myself? Is that what I did, Irk?"

Irk stared at Herbert, then looked over at us nervously like he hoped we didn't just hear what Herbert said. But when he saw that we did, he got angry and turned back to Herbert.

"What *gold* are you talking about?" Irk asked impatiently. "You *have* it all."

"But I don't have the gold that *he* took," Herbert said, pointing directly at me.

"Is that true, Iggy?" Irk asked.

Not sure what to do, I pulled out the gold piece and held it up for Irk to see.

"You've gotta be kidding me," Karen snorted. "Are you so greedy that you can't even let one tiny piece of gold go? That's nuts."

"Yes, I guess it is," Herbert said with one of his scary smiles. "But it's even more nuts for you to get killed over it. So, why don't you just hand it over? It's not like you can spend it here."

"Maybe we just like it," Karen said, taunting him.

"Clearly it's something that *you* have some huge crush on."

"Oh, how I've missed that clever teenage wit of yours," Herbert said with a big fake laugh. "You really are a delight, aren't you? Why don't you just get your little friend there to hand that gold over and I'll see to it that both of you get back home right away."

"Yeah, if it's anything like the last trip you sent us on, I think we'll pass," Karen said, giving Herbert a big insincere smile.

"That wasn't my doing," Herbert said innocently. "You were the ones who tampered with the machine. If you set it to go someplace different, then I can't control where you end up."

"Somehow, I don't believe you," Karen said, stepping toward Herbert.

Herbert looked nervous that Karen was getting so close and signaled to one of his metal guards. The huge creature immediately stepped forward and slammed his heavy iron leg down right in front of Karen, blocking Herbert from her.

"Jeez, you jerk!" Karen yelled as the metal guy's foot stamp echoed through the rock pillars. "You almost crushed me!"

"I'm sorry," Herbert said, peeking his head around the massive metal leg. "You see, the Ortons don't tend to know their own strength. So it's easy to get hurt around them. For example, if I were to ask them to do something like take a small gold piece out of a little boy's hand, chances are they'd bring me both the gold and the arm that was holding it."

I looked at the gold piece I was holding and then tried to imagine life with only one arm. Don't faint, I told myself. That would be extremely embarrassing.

"Look," Irk said, turning to Karen and me. "This guy is crazy. Just give him his gold and then he can go back to where he came from. It's not worth getting hurt over."

And with that, the big metal guy that Herbert called an Orton held his giant metal hand out and waited for me to give him the gold piece. His hand was so huge and jagged that if he just tapped me with it, he'd pretty much knock my head right off of my shoulders.

"I don't know, Iggy," Karen said, clearly intimidated by the huge Orton. "It *is* only one stupid piece of gold. It's not worth us getting killed over."

She was right. It didn't seem worth it.

And yet...

I don't know. There was just something about the way Herbert was acting and looking at the gold piece, like it was the most important thing in the world to him, that made me feel weird about everything. Maybe the guy was addicted to gold the way my Aunt Sue was addicted to chocolate. Maybe the minute he got this last piece he'd suddenly be really nice and joke around with us and help us get home.

Nah. Something was up, and there was no way I was giving him this little piece of gold.

"Forget it," I said as I started to put the gold back in my pocket. "It belongs to this frequency."

For the next couple of seconds, it felt like everything went into slow motion. I saw Herbert's eyes look over at Irk and some silent communication pass between them. And then Irk's frond darted out and snatched the gold piece right out of my hand as it was halfway into my pocket. He held the gold up to Herbert as Karen lunged forward to grab it back.

"Don't you take anything from him!" she yelled, coming to my defense.

Fast as a cobra striking, Irk's other frond shot out and grabbed Karen by the throat, stopping her mid-lunge. Apparently he was gripping her pretty tightly because Karen couldn't move. Her eyes were bugging out like she was having serious trouble breathing.

"Hey, let her go!" I yelled, stepping forward.

Irk swung his face and glared at me, a crazy look in his eye. "Take one more step, Iggy, and I'll crush her throat!"

I stopped and then looked over at Swiff, who was watching all this, completely confused.

"Irk, what are you doing?" she asked oddly.

"Shut up, Swiff!" he yelled. "Everybody just shut up!"

"Good work, palm tree," Herbert said as he stepped out from behind the Orton's leg. "Glad to see somebody has their priorities straight."

Herbert started to reach out for the gold but then Irk quickly pulled it back, still holding Karen by the throat.

"You too, Herbert," Irk said angrily. "Take one more step and I'll kill her."

Herbert looked confused and stopped. Then he gave a little laugh.

"I was going to kill her anyway. Be my guest."

Irk got a panicked look on his face and then stepped away from Herbert, still holding Karen by the throat.

The Ortons behind Herbert moved forward like they were just waiting for the word to kill us all.

"You've gotta send me to California!" Irk suddenly blurted out. "I'm dying here."

"Is that what this is about?" Herbert said with a surprised chuckle. "You didn't have to go through all this. That's easy. Consider it done. Just give me the gold."

Herbert stepped forward and reached out to take the gold.

"Wait," Irk snapped as he stepped back. "You double-crossed me the last time. I want some assurance that you won't do it again."

Herbert sighed and shook his head like he couldn't believe what was happening. "You really don't understand the situation, do you? You have nothing to bargain with. If you don't hand me the gold in two seconds, I'll just have my metal friends here take it from you. You *have* figured that out, right?"

Irk just stood there, holding Karen's throat, looking a bit frozen. He groaned a little and flexed his side as he grimaced in pain. He was not a well tree.

"Look, Irk, clearly you're not yourself today. And I feel bad because of what I did to you last time. But that

little piece of gold means more to me than anything
else in this frequency. So, it was nice knowing you. But
I'll be sure to send your lifeless trunk to California so
they can use it as firewood. That's what we do to trees
in our frequency. We burn them. Now…" Herbert said,
turning to the Ortons, "get my gold."

Herbert signaled to the Ortons as we all started
to back up. Irk let go of Karen's throat as the metal
men stalked toward us. Just as they were about to grab
us…

WHOOSH!

A flash of white swept past my eyes as the gold

piece disappeared out of Irk's hand. We all looked up and saw something that looked like...

Foo?

"Oh, man, I'm hallucinating again," I said, shaking my head. "I just imagined Foo saved us."

"I did too," Karen said.

"Who's that flying meat?" Swiff asked as she stared up at the sky.

I wasn't imagining it. It *was* Foo!

"Foo?" I called up to her. "Is that really you? How did you get here?"

"After you left," she called down, holding the piece of gold in her hand, "I was trying to figure out how to make the machine bring you back and the next thing I knew, I was in Herbert's world where he keeps all his gold. Iggy, we can't let him have any more of it. I heard him talking. He's going to do something terrible with the gold. That's why I followed him here through the machine. We have to stop him, Iggy!"

Before I could even think about what she said, Foo yelled, "Run, Iggy! RUN!"

Karen and I looked up just in time to see the Ortons swinging their hands down to crush us. We immediately bolted off.

BOOM!!!

The Ortons' hands just missed us and hit the ground hard, making it shake like an earthquake.

"Leave them alone!" Foo called down to Herbert as she hovered above the Ortons and we ran for our lives. "*I've* got your gold now!"

"You two!" Herbert called to the Ortons closest to him. "Don't let the flying girl out of your sight. The rest of you, stop the others!"

We ran full speed through the Life is Beautiful Forest and weaved through the rock pillars that we hoped would slow down the Ortons. But the four now chasing us ran straight through the pillars, plowing them down like bowling pins. Boulders and debris rained down around us as the Ortons exploded through each column, their eyes locked on us like laser beams. It was very clear we couldn't outrun them, not all the way back to...

Where?

The plant city? The tree city? Those places were so far away we'd never make it.

BLAM!

The Ortons smashed through another pillar as one of them picked up a huge boulder and threw it.

KA-BOOM!

The boulder hit the ground right behind us and

exploded like a bomb of rock and black ooze, throwing us forward off our feet.

Okay, exactly *how* do we deal with these guys? I wondered as I slid on my face.

I was open to any and all suggestions.

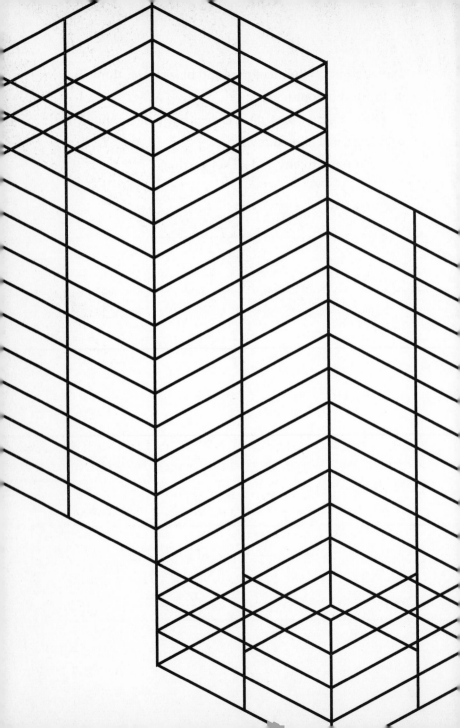

28
I Have an Idea

"Split up!" I yelled as we scrambled to our feet, trying not to slip on the gunky ground. "Run in different directions!"

We hit the gas and fanned out as the four Ortons chased each of us separately.

"Speed up as much as you can!" I yelled.

"What do you think we're *doing*?" Karen yelled as her Orton was almost on top of her. "They're too fast."

"Be faster!" I yelled. "Just for another few seconds."

We all somehow burst into an even faster sprint, the Ortons chugging at top speed on our heels.

"Karen, on three, make a sharp turn and run directly at me!" I called out. "Swiff and Irk, do the same thing with each other."

"Oh, man," Karen yelled, sounding winded for the first time since I'd known her. "I think I know what you're doing and I really hope it works. 'Cause if it doesn't, we're dead."

I threw her a look that said, "If you've got a better idea, I'd love to hear it," and then counted off.

"One...two...THREE!"

Karen and I took sharp 90-degree turns toward each other as Irk and Swiff did the same. The Ortons turned on a dime and rushed after us.

"Faster!" I yelled. "Run right at each other!"

Karen and I were closing the gap fast, our faces straining like baseball players rounding third base. I looked back and saw that my Orton had his eyes locked on me, as if catching me was the only thing in the world he cared about.

Swiff and Irk were on a collision course, too, although

Irk clearly didn't have the super bouncing speed he used to. The lack of dark and sunlight had really taken its toll on him.

And then, right as we were all about to hit head-on, I yelled, "Now!"

Karen and I sidestepped and just missed colliding, our shirt sleeves slapping together as we blew past each other.

KA-BLAM! The Ortons collided full speed. They hit so hard that the entire valley shook from the tons of metal impacting.

We all stopped running and looked back as we tried to catch our breath. The Ortons had practically fused into one, their faces smashed together and their arms and legs tangled up like the strings on the cheap marionette my Uncle Phil brought me back from Tijuana.

With a loud creak, the Ortons slowly cracked apart from each other and fell to the ground, shaking the black goo beneath our feet.

And then they were silent. Totally unconscious.

"Just how I like them," Karen said as she looked at the fallen giants at our feet. "Big and stupid."

I looked up into the sky for Foo. I saw her at the

other end of the forest, high above the two remaining Ortons, who were breaking pieces off of pillars and throwing them at her like cannonballs. Fortunately, she was able to dodge them as she watched to see if we were all right.

"We have to get back to the transporter," Karen said as she stared at Herbert, who was watching us from the mouth of the cave. "Oh, wait, but first…"

Karen turned and punched Irk right in the face.

"*That's* for trying to strangle me!" she said as she spun and roundhouse kicked him right in the trunk. "And *that's* for trying to sell us out *and* for helping Herbert steal the plants' gold in the first place."

Irk fell to the ground, gasping and in pain. Swiff just stared at him and then looked at Karen, unsure how to feel about this attack on her leader.

"I'm sorry," Irk said, crying. "You don't know what it's like. I have nowhere to go. If I stay in the plant city, I can't survive by only drinking dark. If I go to the tree city, they just throw me in jail. But I let them arrest me so I can recharge myself with their sunlight. Then once I'm feeling better, I hate it there so much I have to escape. Then I go back to the plant city and live on dark and get sick and it all starts over again. I'm telling you, I've gotta get to California or I'm gonna die!"

Karen stared at him as he put his head on the ground, pretty much having a breakdown. It was clear she didn't like him anymore, but it was sort of hard to hate him when he was such a blubbering wreck.

"Then we *have* to get back to that transporter," she said as she looked over at Herbert. "I think we *all* need to get out of here."

Just then, more Ortons started coming out of the cave. Five, then another five, then ten more. An army of twenty huge metal soldiers now stood at the other end of the rock forest, staring across at us.

"I think we're gonna need some more help if we want to get back in there," I said.

"Is this all because of that one little piece of gold?" Swiff asked.

"It sure seems like it," said Karen, who then looked down at Irk. "You seem to have a cozy little relationship with Herbert. Do you know anything about this?"

"No," Irk said through his sniffles as he got painfully to his feet. "All I know is that he wanted our gold to 'hide' it from the trees."

Karen and I stared across the forest at the army Herbert had assembled. Foo was still hovering above them as more Ortons threw boulders and rocks at her. I could see her looking over at us, wondering why we weren't running.

"I should have just given him the gold when I had the chance," I said with a sigh. "It's not worth all this. If Foo gets hurt I'll never forgive myself.

"FOO!" I yelled as loud as I could. "Just give the big baby his stupid gold so that he'll go away!"

Foo looked over at me and shook her head no.

And then she flew straight up into the yellow-and-purple clouds and disappeared from sight.

Herbert sighed and shook his head.

"You don't really think it's *this* easy to steal from me, do you?" he yelled up at the clouds. He then turned toward the cave and clapped his hands twice.

Out came what looked like two huge rats. And I mean *huge*. They were each about the size of a minivan and were crawling on their bellies, pulling themselves forward with their spindly front arms and pointy claws. As they came out further, I could see they had three back legs. Two were where the back legs on a normal rat would be but instead of a tail, there was a third, big-

ger leg that looked like a beaver's tail with long sharp
spikes around the edges.

"It figures the big rat would have his own big rats,"
Karen said with a snort.

"What do you think they do?" I asked, feeling really
queasy at the thought of getting chased and eaten by
giant smelly rats.

"I don't know, but as long as they can't fly, they're
not going to help him catch Foo," Karen said.

Herbert put his fingers into his mouth and did a

loud whistle toward the rats. He then pointed up at the clouds and yelled, "Get the girl!"

There was a gross ripping sound like the noise you hear when you lift your foot off a really sticky movie theater floor. Then, the thick wiry black hair on the rats' backs split open and two huge slimy black wings covered with some kind of thick gray snot came out of the opening. The rats extended the wings out and suddenly they looked a lot more like enormous *bats*.

"Holy guacamole..." I heard Karen say under her breath.

The rat/bats started to flap their wings, which sent their wing snot flying all over the place. *BLAP!* A big glob of it hit Herbert Golonski right on the front of his shirt, covering his tie with thick goop. He looked down at it angrily.

"GO!" he yelled at the rats.

With one flap of their wings, the rats took off flying straight up into the clouds like gross, hairy rockets.

"Foo! Look out!" I yelled up at the clouds as the rats disappeared from view. "They're coming to get you!"

"Yell all you want, Mr. MacFarland," Herbert said, trying to sound like a cool villain but looking less than suave because he was daintily wiping off his gooey shirt and tie with a hankerchief. "The Corpulens never miss their targets. In some ways, they are the most dangerous and deadly creatures in any frequency. They have no conscience. They are perfect killing machines. They only know how to hunt and to eat. So, I'm afraid your little flying friend's time is up."

There was a loud *screech* from inside the clouds. Herbert smiled as we all looked up. Was it Foo? Did she just yell in pain? Was that her bird voice she used whenever she got scared or was in danger?

"FOO!" I yelled.

"Oh, well," Herbert said with a chuckle. "I guess that's the end of that."

ZOOM! The two flying rats that I guess were called Corpulens came bursting out of the clouds, screeching and diving straight at us like missiles.

"Did you get the girl?" Herbert yelled up at them. "You better not have swallowed the gold when you ate her."

The Corpulens just kept diving straight down toward us and I could see they had these weird happy looks on their nasty faces. They kept screeching over and over and diving faster and faster and slowly a ratty, crackling voice came out of my translating disc.

"…Food!…Food!"

I followed what their eyes were staring at and saw they were looking right at the ground in the middle of the battlefield. But there was no food anywhere to be seen. Which was when I realized…

"The Good Times gas!" Karen said in disbelief.

Herbert looked from Karen to the Corpulens, then held up his hands and started yelling at them.

"No! Stop! The food's up there! You're seeing things! Wake up and get the girl!"

BLAM!

The two Corpulens smashed straight into the battlefield like missiles. They hit so hard and went so deep into the ground that the only things sticking up out of the dirt were the tips of their wings, their back feet, and their butts.

Herbert and the metal men all stared at the crashed Corpulens as the rats' back legs twitched.

"Are they alive?" Swiff asked, breaking the silence.

BRAAAP! A mushroom cloud of dark green gas blasted out of their butts like a volcano, then their legs went limp like wilted petals on a flower.

"Uh…I'm guessing not," said Karen.

Herbert stared at his dead Corpulens, then glared right at me.

248

"BRING ME IGNATIUS MACFARLAND!" he screamed.

And with that, his army of ten-foot-tall metal men starting running toward me as we turned and ran for our lives.

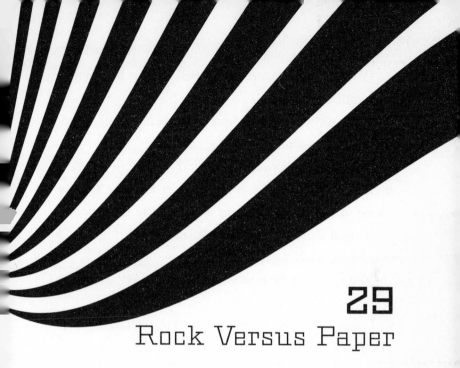

29
Rock Versus Paper

"HALT!"

That's what we heard the minute we burst through the ring of tall mushrooms that surrounded the Life is Beautiful Forest. There in front of us were Yarg and his tough willow-tree wife, Gree, standing before about forty tree soldiers who were all wearing armor and holding weapons.

"Yarg!" I blurted out, never happier to see anyone or anything in my life. "I can't believe you're here!"

"You're all under arrest!" he bellowed as he pointed his sword at us.

"How did you know where we were?" Karen asked, clearly as happy to see the trees as I was.

"We followed you," Yarg said, stepping forward angrily. "One of our patrols saw you heading for the ravine. And unless you were doing a little sightseeing, we figured there was a good chance you just might lead us to our gold."

The ground began to shake as the heavy footsteps of the metal army got closer.

I stepped toward the tree army. "Yarg, you have to—"

"Stay right where you are!" he said threateningly as his army all drew their weapons like I was the biggest danger they were about to confront. "I knew you were not to be trusted. None of your species are. You all lie. And now you will lead us to our gold and then we will lock you away forever."

As Yarg was yelling, the rest of the trees started to look around, confused at the rumbling ground.

"Yarg!" Gree snapped. "Be quiet for a minute."

"Don't tell me to be quiet in front of the prisoners," he snapped back. "I—"

SMASH!

Two metal army guys burst through the ring of mushrooms like speeding trucks, disintegrating them into dust. Yarg's eye went wide as the tree army all jumped back, completely surprised.

"Holy sap!" yelled Yarg as he tried to reach for an axe on his weapons belt. But there was no time.

BLAM!

The two metal guys plowed right into Yarg and Gree, sending them flying back with such force they smashed into the tree army and knocked them all down.

"Oh, man…" was all I could say as the metal guys started running toward me. Karen reached over and grabbed a sword off a tree soldier's belt as I stood frozen in fear.

"Run, boyfriend!" Swiff yelled as she grabbed me by the back of the collar and yanked me off my feet. She started running so fast that all I could do was drag along behind her. I thought that Karen would follow us but instead she turned toward the metal guys and cocked her sword back like a baseball bat.

"Karen!" I yelled as I slid away from her. "Get out of there!"

"I've had enough of these guys!" she yelled over her shoulder.

CLANG! Karen swung her sword into the front metal guy's leg so hard that it folded under him and he plowed face first into the ground. The guys running behind him were too close and so they all tripped over him and wiped out.

"Swiff, stop!" I yelled as I saw the Ortons look over at Karen and start to get up. "We've got to get her out of there."

Swiff looked back and saw Karen brandish her sword again as the metal guys started to stalk toward her.

"I'll save her!" Swiff yelled as she dashed off toward Karen. "You stay here!"

Swiff flew through the air and landed on the back of the Orton who was closest to Karen. She tried to wrap herself around his knees to trip him but he just moved his leg forward and Swiff lost her grip.

"Swiff, get off him!" Karen yelled, her sword up and ready for a fight. "I can't hit him without chopping you in half!"

"I'll take care of him!" Swiff hollered as she climbed onto the Orton's back and started pounding her leaves against his hard metal body, having no effect on him whatsoever.

An Orton behind her saw Swiff and threw a huge punch at her.

"Look out!" yelled Karen.

Swiff saw the Orton's fist coming and jumped out of the way just in time.

BOOM!

He punched his fellow Orton in the back so hard that the guy stumbled forward, then spun around to see what hit him. He saw the guy behind him with his fist still clenched, then reared back and punched the guy right in the chest.

And the next thing we knew, all the metal guys were in a huge brawl.

BOOM! BAM! PLAM!

The whole ravine shook as they punched and kicked each other like a bunch of Statues of Liberty having a street fight.

"Karen!" I yelled. "Grab Swiff and get out of there!"

If I had thought Karen liked to fight, she was nothing compared to the crazy daisy. Swiff, who was standing next to the fighting metal men with her fists clenched, looked like she was trying to figure out the best time to leap into the boxing match.

"C'mon, flower girl," Karen said, grabbing Swiff by the middle of her stem. "We'll need your help getting out of here."

"I don't run away from any fight!" Swiff yelled as she struggled to get out of Karen's grip.

BOOM!

Two of the Ortons smashed their chests together like two speeding train engines hitting head on.

"This is *definitely* one fight to run from," Karen said as Swiff stopped struggling, clearly doing the math of daisy girl versus enormous metal man army equals dead flower.

"Maybe you're right," Swiff said as we all took off running.

The metal army looked and saw the three of us trying to escape. The head Orton raised his arms out to the side as if to say "Stop" to the others. They immediately quit fighting and started to run after us again.

"Oh, man, we're so dead," I yelled.

The head Orton bolted up behind Karen and Swiff, his hand raised to slap down and squash them flat.

"Crush them," I heard a deep rumble say from my translating disc.

And that was when I heard a big *CLANG*!

I turned and saw the Orton go flying sideways.

CLANG! CLANG! CLANG!

More of the metal army was sent flying off their feet.

Karen, Swiff, and I turned and saw Yarg, Gree, and the rest of the tree patrol standing in battle formation, having just flung their axes.

"If you're looking to crush something," Yarg said to the Orton army in a super scary voice, "then why don't you try to crush us?"

A huge battle began. The trees were swinging their axes and swords and other dangerous metal blades, and the metal guys were using their huge arms and legs to fight back at the trees.

Unfortunately, it didn't look very good for the trees.

The Ortons were just too strong. They were made out of solid metal and everyone knows that metal is pretty much stronger than wood. So, the trees were getting their butts kicked big time.

"Iggy! C'mon!" Karen yelled as I saw an Orton get a huge maple tree in a bear hug and then twist him sideways, shattering his trunk into an explosion of splinters. "They're fighting the Ortons so we can escape!"

"Escape to where?" I yelled back.

"Anywhere but here!" she answered.

"Run, Iggy!" Yarg's voice hollered through my translator. "Get back to the tree city! Tell the—"

SMASH!

The Orton fighting with Yarg took advantage of his momentary loss of focus and hit him full force right in the head. Yarg grunted in pain and fell sideways. The Orton then jumped up and started to run toward me. I looked past him and saw that Herbert Golonski had just entered the battlefield from the Life is Beautiful Forest and was seeing the fight for the first time. He yelled, "Don't let Ignatius get away!"

Before the Orton could grab me, something flew through the air and leaped onto its back.

It was Gree. And, man, was she mad.

"I'll teach you to hurt my husband!" she yelled as she whipped a huge spiky axe off her back and swung it over her head and straight down into the Orton's chest.

SWACK!

She hit the guy so hard that the axe stuck deep into his rib cage. He stopped running and just stood there, frozen. Did Gree kill him?

After a moment, the metal guy quickly reached over his head, grabbed Gree by her willowy hair, and flipped her forward the way a guy at a carnival swings a huge hammer down onto one of those "Test Your Strength" games.

SLAM!

Gree hit the ground so hard that the impact knocked me off my feet.

"GREE!" Yarg yelled, trying to stand up but clearly in too much pain.

The metal guy then swung Gree over his head the other way and slammed her down even harder as a loud *crack* came out of her trunk and she moaned in pain.

"NO!" Yarg yelled as he struggled to get up. But another Orton came over to Yarg and picked him up like a barbell. He lifted Yarg high over his head and put up his knee, ready to break him in half.

This had gone too far. Trying to protect that stupid piece of gold wasn't worth getting anyone killed, especially not someone good like Yarg.

"*STOP!*" I yelled at the top of my lungs as I held my hands up high. "I'll give you the gold! Just please don't kill anybody!"

The guy holding Yarg over his head froze. The Orton about to flip Gree again stopped too, as did all the other metal guys who were about to destroy the tree army.

Then they all turned and looked back at Herbert.

"If you don't get the flying girl to bring back that gold right now, I'm going to kill everyone here," Herbert said loudly but calmly from the other side of the battlefield.

"FOO!" I called up at the clouds. "Come down and give him the gold!"

"Iggy, no!" Karen yelled. "The minute he gets that gold, he's going to kill them anyway."

I stared at Karen, then turned back to Herbert.

"Will you really kill them?"

"Only if I don't get that gold immediately," he said. "If I do, I'll leave you all alone and take my army with me."

260

"Oh, *please*," Karen said with a snort. "He's lying, Iggy."

"Are you lying?" I called back to him.

"No, you have my word," he said stepping forward. "I am not a liar. But the clock is ticking. And quickly."

I looked up at the clouds again but Foo was nowhere to be seen.

"Foo!" I yelled. "Please come down! It's okay. I *want* to give him the gold!"

We all stared up at the clouds. Waiting.

But no Foo.

Where was she?

I did see her earlier, right?

Oh, man, I thought. I sure hope it wasn't just another hallucination.

"Tick tock, Mr. MacFarland," Herbert said as he stared over at me. Then I saw him make a small nod of his head to the Orton next to him. The metal guy started walking toward me slowly.

"Iggy, get out of there!" Karen yelled.

"No," I said, holding my ground.

"He's just going to kill you," she called, panic in her voice.

"No, he's not," I called back. "Because if he does, Foo will never give him his gold back."

Completely certain that I was right, I stared at the metal man as he walked right up to me and stood looking down as if I were a tiny bug he was deciding whether or not to step on and flatten like a penny on a train track.

I did everything I could not to faint as I stared up into the black slit between his shoulders that seemed to be what Ortons used as eyes.

The Orton looked at Herbert, then turned back and before I knew what happened, he reached out and grabbed me with his huge hard metal hand.

Gee, I thought. Maybe Herbert Golonski *is* a liar.

30
Herbert Golonski
Sucks

"All right, *Foo*," Herbert yelled up at the clouds, saying Foo's name like he thought it was the dumbest word in the world. "Bring me that gold right now or your boyfriend dies."

"Oh, man, I *knew* that was going to happen!" Karen said as she slapped her forehead.

"Iggy!" Swiff yelled as she started to run toward me. Thankfully, Karen grabbed her stem and stopped her.

"Irk! Do something!" Swiff yelled as I saw him

standing off to the side looking helpless and holding his trunk like whatever pain he was in was only getting worse.

"There's nothing to be done," Herbert said. Irk just stared at Swiff with a look that said he had no idea what to do. Then Herbert looked back up at the clouds again. "All right, Foo. Iggy dies in three...two..."

"NO!" Karen yelled as she ran to help me. But two Ortons quickly jumped forward and landed in front of her.

"I already told her to give you the gold, Herbert!" I yelled. "Killing me isn't going to do anything."

"Actually, it will. It'll get you out of my life."

He then looked back up at the sky and continued his countdown.

"Two... *one*..."

Oh, man. What a way to go. Crushed like an empty soda can.

I had to do something.

"There's more gold in the tree city!" I yelled at the top of my lungs.

Herbert stopped his countdown and looked over at me.

"That's a lie," he said as he gave me a look like the one my dad used to give me when I'd tell him there was a monster living under my bed. "Trust me. I took it all."

"Well, then they were hiding some from you because I saw it two days ago when they were interrogating me. A big pile of it in a secret room. They don't even know that I saw it but I did."

Okay, obviously I was lying. And I know I'm not supposed to lie. But I figured if the difference between telling a lie and not telling a lie at that moment was whether Karen, Swiff, and I would live or die, lying didn't exactly seem like the worst thing I could do.

And I had a plan. I swear.

"If you take us back to the tree city," I said, "I'll get you that gold. But only if you promise to just take it, leave the trees alone, and take Karen and me with you back to our frequency."

"I wouldn't say that you're in much of a position to bargain with me," Herbert said. "If what you're saying is true, I could just kill all of you and then get this alleged gold from the city myself."

"You can't get into the city, even with your metal army," I said back, trying to act the way I had always seen guys in movies act when they're bargaining with the bad guy. "The place can't be broken into. But I can make them open it for you. Then I'll get you your gold."

I looked over at Yarg, who looked back at me, confused. I stared at him and put all my energy into my eyes, hoping that somehow I could communicate to go along with me on this.

Fortunately, Yarg was a really smart guy.

"Traitor!" he yelled at me, super angry. "We will give him nothing!"

"You have to, Yarg," I said back to him. "They'll kill you if you don't."

"Then they can kill us!" he yelled. "We would rather die than give you and your species one more ounce of our gold."

And with that, Yarg jumped up and ran at me like he was going to kill me. An Orton threw his huge arm out to the side and caught Yarg right across his face. Yarg's roots flew out from under him and he slammed down hard on his back. He then jumped back up and tried to charge at me again. Another Orton grabbed him from behind and held him in a tight bear hug as Yarg thrashed around like crazy.

"I'll kill you, you traitor!" he screamed at me, his eye red with anger. "I'LL KILL YOU!!!"

Man alive, I thought. Yarg is a really good actor.

At least I hoped he was acting.

Herbert studied his army and the trees, then glanced back toward the cave where the transporter was, like he was trying to figure out whether he believed me or not.

This has to work, I told myself. My plan was to get us all back to the underground city where I figured, the tree army could bring out all their weapons and dangerous vehicles and more than outnumber and overpower the Orton army.

We could capture Herbert and make him take us back to our frequency, where we could then send the gold back to this world and have Herbert locked up for being such a bad guy. And then I'd be done with all this crazy frequency jumping. It had been a pretty cool adventure but I was ready to see my parents, sleep in my own bed, and have a hamburger and French fries all without having someone constantly trying to kill me. Because that was getting really annoying.

Herbert finally sighed and said impatiently, "All right. Let's just do this."

He then nodded at the Orton army. They reached

down and picked up all the tree soldiers and Irk. At the same time, the two other Ortons grabbed Karen and Swiff and snatched them off the ground.

"You're digging into my ribs, you big pile of junk!" Karen gasped as she tried to break free of the Orton's hands but couldn't. She was trapped and, as I was finding out, the more you struggled against the grip of a jagged metal hand, the more you hurt *yourself* and not the hand.

Swiff, however, was just too thin and wiry for her Orton to hold and she slipped out of his grasp like an angry snake. She jumped onto my Orton and frantically tried to pull his arms apart to free me.

"Let go of my boyfriend!" Swiff yelled as she wrapped and unwrapped herself around various parts of his jagged metal body.

"Just put us down, Herbert," I said as Swiff started kicking the Orton in his rocky shins with her roots.

"If you want to go back to the tree city, then this is how we get you there," Herbert said as a big Orton next to him reached down and then, much more gently than any of the metal men did for the rest of us, picked him up.

Seeing that this was how Herbert wanted to transport us all back through the ravine and across the long

distance that we would have had to walk, I realized that my plan might actually be working.

"Put him *down*, you jerk!" Swiff yelled as she continued to pound on my Orton.

Well, I meant my plan was working except for the part that didn't figure on having a slightly insane but well-meaning flower trying to save me and potentially ruin everything.

And it was at that moment that I realized I needed to get rid of Swiff.

31
HE LOVES ME,
HE LOVES ME NOT

"Swiff!" I yelled in the angriest voice I could muster. "*Stop it!*"

"What's the matter, boyfriend?" she asked me, looking confused. "I'm trying to save you."

"I don't need saving!" I yelled, super meanly. "Why don't you just leave me alone?"

Swiff looked very thrown at what I said and the tone of my voice. She blinked her big eye and stared at me.

"But you're in danger," she said quietly. "Don't you want me to help you?"

Her voice sounded so sad and hurt that I felt like just telling her I was sorry and letting her come with us. But I knew that there was too much chance of her getting hurt or killed since she just couldn't stop herself from fighting Ortons and trying to protect me. And so the only way I could save her was by making her hate me so much that she'd stop caring about me.

"I don't want your help, I don't want to hear your voice and I don't want to see your face," I said coldly. "You're annoying, and everything you do only makes things worse. So why don't you just go back to your stupid city with all the rest of your stupid species and leave us alone?"

Swiff just stared at me in total shock. The irony was that everything I said was how I actually felt when I first met her. I had wanted to say those words to her a lot in the last few days and yet now that I said it and saw how sad it made her, I realized I didn't mean any of it.

It's easy to act as if you don't like someone who really really likes you because you figure they'll like you no matter what. But the minute they stop liking you, you realize that you actually *do* like them and then try to do everything you can to get them to like you again.

Well, the way Swiff was staring at me like I had just torn out her heart, and stomped on it like a school janitor smashing garbage into a trashcan with his foot, I got hit with such a wave of regret, I almost started to cry. But to do that would only ruin everything. And so I just stared back at her with the meanest face I could make.

Swiff's eye slowly filled with anger as all her petals tightened, pointing at me like a circle of angry fingers. She looked so scary that I immediately went from feeling bad to being terrified she was going to kill me. I guess I forgot that an angry Swiff was a dangerous Swiff.

"*YOU'RE* STUPID!" she yelled in my face, practically blowing out the speaker in my translating disc. "Why don't *you* go back to *your* stupid world and leave all of *us* alone?!"

And with that, she jumped down off the Orton who

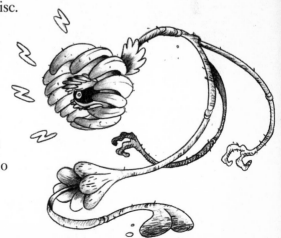

was holding me and landed on the ground in front of Irk's metal man.

"C'mon, Irk, let's get out of here."

Irk stared at her with a tired, fed-up eye. Either he knew he had to do the same thing I had just done or he really felt this way. But from the tone of voice in which he said the following sentences, it seemed pretty clear that he wasn't acting.

"Swiff, just go home and don't bother any of us ever again. Iggy's right. You *are* annoying."

Swiff turned and looked at Karen, who just looked down to avoid her eye. Then Swiff gave me a last look, turned a cold eye to Herbert, and said, "I hope you destroy them all."

And then she ran off out of the ravine.

Well, Swiff was safe, but now *I* felt terrible.

32
The Short Long
Ride Home

Okay, if earlier during my time in this frequency I
thought that getting carried by trees was the most painful thing I'd ever felt, then I'm here to tell you I had no
idea what I was talking about. Because getting carried
by a tree was like lying in a big feather bed compared
to getting carried by a guy made out of metal who was
running about fifty miles an hour.

Herbert's Orton army was on the move and it looked
like it was a pretty painful event for everyone involved.

Karen was getting the same rough treatment as I was, since her Orton was holding her with both hands like she was a baseball bat he was about to swing. Her face was grimacing in pain, and I guess mine was too because when we looked at each other, neither of us bothered to say anything.

Behind us, the rest of the Ortons were running along, each tightly carrying a member of the tree army. Herbert said back in the ravine that he wanted to bring all the "hostages" along so that he'd have some "insurance" in case anybody in the tree city tried to double-cross him. This, of course, was complicating my plan terribly, and yet for some reason I figured that if we could just get to the underground city, something positive could happen.

Okay, I know what you're thinking. This was a really lame plan. Hey, I'm only twelve and a half years old. The only class I've ever gotten any grade better than a C in was art and I don't think knowing how to make a paper turkey out of my handprint is exactly going to turn me into a military mastermind. But at least I was getting us closer to an army that might be able to help us.

I kept looking up at the sky to see if Foo was anywhere to be seen. But with all the rain and clouds up there, it was impossible to tell if she had even made it out of the fog over the ravine. I had to think her brain was smart enough not to fall for whatever the gas would throw at her. And yet Karen, who was about the smartest person I had ever met, had been fooled by the gas as badly as I had. Maybe no one was immune. I think the only reason none of us had hallucinated on the way out of the ravine was because the Ortons had run so fast that there wasn't time for the fog to get into our brains.

Herbert suddenly raised his arms and the Ortons skidded to a stop. He flew forward and almost fell out of his Orton's hands. But he stopped himself, his face down and his butt sticking up in the air, looking momentarily like Ivan's baby brother when he would take a nap. Herbert then flipped over and jumped up, trying to act like his embarrassing fall onto his face hadn't just happened.

"All right, Ignatius MacFarland," he said really loudly, like he was making a speech to the entire world. "Go get me my gold."

He gestured to the ground in front of us and I saw the big crack that indicated the sliding door entrance to the tree city. The Orton holding me opened his hands and let me drop five feet to the ground. I hit the muddy, rain-soaked sludge and fell right on my face. I looked up at Herbert, who made a really fake surprised expression and said "Oops."

What a jerk.

Herbert looked over at the Orton holding Yarg and nodded. The metal man tossed Yarg onto the ground, making him land on his back. Yarg groaned in pain and then struggled to get up. He was in pretty bad shape after his battle with the Ortons. But he was trying hard to hide it.

"I will not open my city to you or anyone else," Yarg said as he stared angrily at Herbert.

"Oh, I think you will," Herbert said back as he raised his hand and snapped his finger.

The Orton holding Gree raised her up over his head and lifted one knee.

"If you don't get me that gold right now, I'll break her in half."

Herbert then snapped his fingers again and the Orton holding Karen tightened his grip on Karen's body, making her squeak in pain, unable to even talk.

"And if *you* don't get Yarg to do what you say," Herbert said, staring right at me, "I'll twist your girlfriend in half."

Even though Karen clearly wasn't my girlfriend, I got the message. Herbert meant business and now my plan was definitely looking like something I really hadn't thought through.

Yarg looked at Gree, who seemed to be in so much pain she couldn't talk, then glared at Herbert. He then gave a long angry sigh and walked over to the tree city door. As he raised his leg and was about to stomp down to signal the trees inside to open it, Herbert called out.

"Oh, and if you give the secret code of two quick stomps, a pause, and then one more stomp, which tells the city to scramble its full army because there's an enemy force outside, I'll also break your wife in half."

Yarg looked over at Herbert and then slowly put his leg back down. Herbert sighed and shook his head.

"And if you get any ideas once you get inside, you should know that it is physically impossible for your city to defeat my Orton army. We will easily destroy all of you."

Yarg stared at Herbert, then let out a loud laugh of his own.

"You can't be serious," Yarg said as he stepped toward Herbert. "You think twenty metal men can defeat our full forces? You can kill me and kill Gree but my army will brush the few of you aside as if you were the steel girders we bend to our will every day."

Herbert made a face to show that he was impressed with Yarg's attitude. Then he nodded his head as if he was admitting Yarg was right.

"You know what, Yarg? It's true that twenty Ortons might not be able to defeat your army. But five hundred would utterly destroy every last one of you."

And that was when we heard the faint rumbling.

I strained my eyes to see where it was coming from. I then saw a long shiny line breaking through the distant rain. As I looked closer, I could see it was a huge army of metal guys all running toward us at top speed. And from the look of things, I'd have to say there were indeed five hundred of them.

"Now," said Herbert as he turned back to Yarg and me. "I'd open that door and get my gold or I'll have my army tear the roof right off your city."

Yarg watched as the five hundred new metal men ran up and stopped in a huge formation behind the twenty original Ortons, one of which was holding his wife, ready to snap her in half. Yarg was clearly trying to figure out what to do. But by the look of the endless sea of huge metal fighters now facing him, it was clear there was nothing any of us *could* do.

Oh, man, I thought. Just wait until Herbert finds out there's no gold in that city. This was a really bad plan.

Yarg turned to Herbert, narrowed his eye and said, "Not even five hundred of your men can pry this door open. It is impenetrable. So, you might as well kill all of us up here because I am not letting any of you into my city."

That was it. We were dead. And there was nothing I could say to Yarg to make him change his mind.

Because he was right.

I couldn't pretend that a few of us up here getting killed was worse than an entire city of living beings getting wiped out.

And so all I could do was try to make sure that Herbert and his army left the tree city alone and just got out of this frequency.

"Herbert…there's no gold in that city," I said, stepping forward and actually feeling proud of myself for one of the few times in my life. "I made it up just so you'd get us out of the ravine."

Herbert looked at me for a few seconds and it was hard to tell what he was thinking. At least I felt good about having briefly fooled a really smart but evil guy like Herbert Golonski. Or at least I did until he said super sarcastically…

"Gee, *really?*"

Uh-oh.

"I *know* there's no gold in the tree city," he continued. "Like I told you, I *took* it all the last time I was here."

He then pulled out a small flat piece of what looked like glass and held it up. It had a bunch of alien-looking numbers and grids on it and one small little light flashing in the center.

"This shows me where all the gold in this frequency is and the only bit of it," he said, pointing at the flashing light, "is up in the sky with your little flying friend."

"Then why did you let us bring you all the way back here?" I asked, my stomach suddenly feeling like it was filled with really heavy rocks.

"Because this frequency has always been more trouble than it's worth. And so for me to continue my work here, I need to get rid of the tree people once and for all. Which is exactly what I am going to do right now. And we can either do it the hard way," he said as he pointed at his enormous Orton army, "or the easy way."

And with this, he signaled toward his metal troops. Several of them stepped forward, each holding huge metal canisters in their hands. When I looked closer, I couldn't believe my eyes.

They were canisters of tree killing gas!

Yarg stared at the shiny containers, not knowing what they were. But he could tell from Karen's and my faces that whatever they were, they were really bad.

"You can't do this, Herbert," Karen yelled as she struggled to break free of the Orton's hands, which was impossible. "It's too much. You got enough gold from this frequency. Just go back home and leave them alone. How much gold do you need?!"

"From this frequency? Not much more," he said flatly. "In fact, I had all that I needed until you and your friends stole it from me."

"We didn't steal anything," I said, getting mad. "That little piece we found was something you dropped. You had forgotten all about it until we picked it up."

"I didn't forget about it," he said, staring right at me with a scary look on his face. "And if you hadn't taken it, I wouldn't be here right now and the tree people would be living their lives and everything would be the way it always was."

"Yeah, with them stuck in a war with the plants because you made them think they had stolen each other's gold," Karen snapped.

"Hey, the way I look at it," Herbert said with a

chuckle, "I just gave them something to do with their lives. Everyone needs a hobby. But now, thanks to you two, their fun must come to an end. And so, would somebody like to open the door to the city or should I just have the Ortons rip it off?"

"I already told you," Yarg growled at Herbert. "That door is impenetrable. The entire city is."

"He's telling the truth," a voice said.

We all looked over and saw that it was Irk. He was being held up by one of the Ortons. His fronds were very wilted and the color of his trunk had gone from its usual tan color to a sort of sick-looking gray. He hung from the Orton's hand like an old stalk of celery that had been in the refrigerator way past its freshness date. But there was something in his eye that said he had a new reason to feel healthy. It was the look of somebody who had an idea.

A terrible idea.

33
Irk's Terrible Idea

"The tree city *is* impenetrable," Irk continued, his voice weak but growing stronger with each word. "One thousand Ortons couldn't damage it. It was built to withstand any and all attacks. *But* there is a secret way to open it from the outside. When it was first designed, a safety latch was hidden up here in case someone needed to make an emergency entrance. You know, if enemy forces ever took over the city and controlled it from the inside. Once this latch is engaged, it overrides all the controls inside the city. They can't close the doors. They'll be completely exposed."

I looked over at Yarg to see his reaction and saw his eye momentarily fill with fear. But the minute he saw me looking, he quickly covered.

"What kind of lie is this?" Yarg said to Irk with a shake of his head. "Lack of sun has finally made you delusional."

"If he's so delusional," Herbert said, giving Yarg a very suspicious look, "then what's the harm in letting him finish what he's saying?"

"Because what he's saying is not true," Yarg said back with a forced laugh.

"I'll be the judge of that," said Herbert as he turned back to Irk.

"I know where that secret latch is and how it works," Irk said, "and I'll show you where it is and how to use it if you promise to take me to California."

"Oh my god," Karen said, disgusted. "You'd sell out your own people and guarantee their deaths just so you can live out some stupid dream in a place you know nothing about? You're pathetic."

"*Like any of us should care about them?!*" Irk yelled at Karen as he pointed to Yarg. "You think they care about *us*? Do you know how many of my people they've killed? You don't think they'd give anything to destroy me and everyone in *my* city?"

"But you're a tree, not a plant!" Karen shouted back. "And trees destroy plants because the plants attack their city and try to destroy *them*. And it's all because of Herbert."

"Things were bad *before* Herbert," Irk said with a sneer. "Trust me. You weren't here. You don't know."

"Well, then it's time for a change," I blurted out, suddenly frustrated with everyone and everything. First, Karen and I got stranded in some stupid frequency we didn't even want to be in. Then we got stuck in the middle of some stupid war that nobody should have been fighting in the first place. And now we were about to get killed because of some stupid gold that nobody even needed.

"Irk, you guys know the trees didn't take your gold and now the trees know that the plants didn't take theirs. So you can all just sit down and work out your differences. Then you can go back and live in the tree city and get the sunlight you need and everybody can try to get along."

"And that's a beautiful sentiment," Herbert said in a tone that told me the next thing he said was going to say started with the word *but*. "*But* unfortunately having the trees here ruins *my* plans. And that doesn't work for *me*. So, I have no choice. The party's over."

Herbert gave me a really annoying smile that said he was super proud of himself and that he thought he was really clever in his evilness and it just made me madder.

"Shut up, you loser!" I snapped at him.

"Excuse me?" he said, not pleased.

"You heard me. Why don't you and your dumb army just go away and leave us all alone? Everyone here's got enough problems without you and you don't need any more gold. You don't have to kill anyone to keep what you have, so just do us all a favor and go back to your frequency and drop dead."

Herbert stared at me, looking like he had no idea what to do or say.

"You'd better watch how you talk to me, boy," Herbert finally said, looking mad.

"Or what? You'll kill me?" I blurted back. "I already know you're going to no matter what I do, especially now that Irk the jerk is going to open the city for you. So why should I watch how I talk to you? You've done nothing but terrible things since the moment I met you. You would have killed me in the last frequency if the cat hadn't attacked you! So why in the world would I ever worry about watching how I talk to you, you stupid freakin' moron?!"

"Because," Herbert said, stepping forward, "you're only hurting your friend."

Herbert gestured over at Karen, who was still being held tightly by the Orton. She couldn't do anything but look back at me with eyes that showed she was more than a little freaked out, which really made me lose it.

"PUT HER DOWN NOW!" I yelled at the Orton holding Karen. I yelled it so loudly and forcefully that the metal man turned and looked at me, then over at Herbert to see if he actually should put her down.

Herbert shook his head "no" at the Orton. I walked up to the Orton and said it again.

"I said, put her down *now*!"

CLANG!

I kicked the Orton in the shin and almost broke my foot.

"OW!" I yelled as I hopped around holding my toe.

Herbert gave me a look like I was crazy, then turned to Irk, who was still being held by his Orton.

"Just open the door," he said to Irk as he gestured to the Orton to put Irk down. Then he rubbed his forehead in pain. "Uch, these lower frequencies give me such a headache."

"You promise to take me to California?" Irk asked Herbert as the Orton set him on the ground.

"You have my word," Herbert said.

"Don't do it, Irk!" I shouted as he headed away from us toward wherever the hidden latch was.

"No!" yelled Yarg as he started to run toward Irk.

SMASH!

Irk's Orton jumped forward and swung his arm right across Yarg's chest. Yarg flew off his feet and landed flat on his back.

Seeing Yarg down, I knew I had to do something and so I ran after Irk. And before I knew what I was doing, I found myself flying through the air with my leg out in front of me like I'd seen Bruce Lee do in an old kung fu movie I watched over at Gary's house. My foot slammed into Irk's back, which sent him flying forward. He landed on his face, then looked back at me with mud dripping off his head. He got an angry look as he lifted himself off the ground with his fronds.

"You are gonna regret that," Irk said as he charged

toward me. Just as he threw a running punch at me, I remembered the technique he and Karen had taught me about using someone's strength against them and being like water flowing around a rock. And so I side-stepped, grabbed his frond, and threw him past me, which made him stumble over his roots. He smashed into the ground and rolled several feet through the mud.

I looked over at Karen, whose eyes showed she was pretty impressed. Then I saw Irk raise himself up on his fronds, shake his head like he couldn't believe what just happened, and look directly at me. If he was upset before, now he was really mad.

"You don't know *anything* about *any* of this!" he yelled at me. "So stay out of it!"

"I know that what you're doing is wrong," I yelled back. "And I'm not going to let you open that city."

"What, I teach you a couple of moves and you think you can beat me? That's a laugh."

"If it's such a laugh, why don't you try and tell me another joke?" I said, feeling more confident than I ever had in my life because I knew what I was doing was right.

Irk jumped up, charged forward...and proceeded to

beat the crap out of me. I tried desperately to use some more of the water-flowing-around-rocks techniques but now I was just a soft rock that Irk was pounding like a sledgehammer.

Yarg jumped up and ran over to the tree city door. He stomped his foot down in the secret code of two quick stomps, a pause, and then one more stomp. Herbert looked over and shook his head.

"So now we have to do this the hard way, do we?" he said with a sigh as we could hear a muffled siren from inside the tree city beneath our feet.

Herbert turned to the Orton army and whistled once. The earth began to shake as all five hundred of them ran forward and got into attack position along the crack in the ground where the city's door would soon be opening. As tough as I knew the trees were, seeing five hundred huge metal men waiting to tear them apart made me realize that the trees didn't stand a chance.

"Irk!" Herbert yelled. "Never mind fighting with the boy. Just open the door."

Irk looked over at Herbert, then picked me up and threw me as far away from everything as he could.

SLAM!

I hit the ground hard and rolled like a rag doll

through the mud, my head smashing into the slop over and over. I didn't break any bones but was pretty sure that if I was alive long enough to go to sleep that night, I'd be waking up extremely sore.

Irk ran and dove onto the ground. He punched his frond down into the mud and dug deep, so that half his head was submerged in the muck. His face strained as he grabbed onto something and tried to turn it.

"Go ahead and let him open it, Herbert," Yarg said from the ground where he was still lying in pain and holding his sore chest. "My army's ready and no matter how indestructible you think your metal men are, there's no way they can defeat our entire city. If I were you, I'd be happy with the gold you already took from us and go back where you came from."

Herbert stared at Yarg for a second, then seemed to deflate a bit.

"You think I enjoy any of this?" Herbert said with a sigh. "It's nothing personal, Yarg. I could care less about you or your people. I have no animosity against any of you. This is just something that has to be done."

"Gee, I'm sure that makes them feel *so* much better," Karen said with a snort. "It's always nice to know that the person killing you is doing it for a good cause."

Irk suddenly grunted loudly as he yanked something upward.

KA-KLANK!

There was a jolt and then the huge door to the city
started to slowly slide open.

"I told you I could do it!" Irk yelled, looking over at
Herbert like he was expecting him to be all "Wow, Irk,
you're the greatest!"

Herbert just shook his head and forced a really
insincere smile that said he thought Irk was a weasel.

"I don't know why you think you have to do this,
nor do I care," Yarg said to Herbert. "All I know is that I
have to protect my people, just as you apparently have
to protect your gold or whatever it is you're protecting.
I wish I could say that I bear no animosity toward you,
but I do. You stole our gold. You plunged us into war.
And now you want to destroy us. If it is a fight you want,
then so be it. But I would ask that at the very least you
let it be a fair fight. No poison, no hostages. You let my
wife and my fighters rejoin our forces and we settle this
with honor. Will you at least agree to that?"

We all turned and stared at Herbert, wondering
what he would do. In the short time I'd known him,
he'd never done anything the fair way. He was the

extreme version of Kyle Showalter, this kid in my class who always cheated at any game you played with him. And if he couldn't cheat, he'd just change all the rules and accuse *you* of cheating. We always called Kyle "The Sore Loser" but he seemed like the best sport in the world compared to Herbert Golonski.

Herbert looked over at Gree, who was up over the head of the Orton holding her. She looked back at him, trying to be tough but clearly helpless and scared. Herbert turned back to Yarg.

"I don't have time," Herbert said with a shake of his head.

He nodded at Gree's Orton.

And that was when the metal man brought his arms up and then started to whip Gree's body down quickly toward his uplifted knee to break her in half.

34
The Early Go

In a flash, Yarg dove toward the Orton and crashed full force into his chest, which knocked the metal guy off balance, since he was only standing on one leg. The fall made him lose his grip, and Gree flew out of his hands and rolled onto the ground.

Another Orton rushed toward Yarg. Yarg jumped up and spun to face the oncoming attacker. The Orton balled up his big metal fist and took a running swing at Yarg. But at the last second Yarg sidestepped and the Orton flew past him and crashed into Gree's Orton, who was just getting up, sending them both sprawling onto the ground.

"Gree! Tell the army what to prepare for!" Yarg yelled as he ran toward Irk. "I'll try to get the door closed."

Gree quickly jumped up and ran to the door that continued to slide open. I expected the Orton army to rush forward and into the opening, but they just stood there, watching. Gree disappeared through the door as it opened wider and wider, exposing more of the city inside. I could see the trees scrambling to put on their armor and man the battle vehicles. This was going to be one huge fight if Yarg couldn't get that door closed again.

Irk saw Yarg running toward him and hit his fighting stance.

"It's too late," Irk yelled at him. "There's nothing you can do. And I won't let you touch this latch."

Yarg didn't even say anything as he kept running at Irk. Irk readied himself even though it was clear he wasn't in very good shape to fight someone huge like Yarg. But there was a look in his eye that said he could practically taste California and his escape from this frequency. And it was clear he didn't want to give that up.

Yarg swung his branch arm at Irk, who ducked it and then jumped on Yarg's back, wrapping his fronds around the giant tree's neck. Irk swung out the bottom of his trunk and then hammered Yarg hard in the back. Yarg stumbled forward, then reached over his head and grabbed Irk's top fronds. He yanked with all his might and threw Irk about fifty yards. Before Irk even landed, Yarg dropped to his knees and plunged his branch into the mud. He quickly found the latch and shoved it down hard.

KA-CHUNK!

The giant door suddenly stopped opening. Yarg pushed down again and the door started to slide shut.

"Attack the city now!" Irk yelled. "The door's going to shut!"

"No, it's not," Herbert said calmly. He then turned to the Ortons and motioned with his head.

Ten Ortons ran to the edge of the opening and hung themselves over the side by one arm and one leg, then straightened out so that they were horizontal like Superman flying. They each put their foot on the head of the Orton behind them, becoming one long

metal brace that was going to stop the door from closing further.

CLANK.

The door hit the first Orton's head and ground to a stop. It whirred and groaned as it tried to close more but the line of Ortons was too strong.

"Okay, now open the valves on the canisters and toss them in," Herbert called out to the Ortons holding the tree-killing poison.

"No!" Yarg shouted as he tried to stand up.

All of a sudden we heard another rumble. I turned and saw that coming over the horizon was a long whirling line of leaves and vines.

It was the plant army. And it looked even bigger than the last time it had attacked the tree city.

"Yeah!" Irk cheered as the Ortons turned to look at

the approaching plants. "*That's* what I'm talking about, baby!"

"Oh, now what?" Herbert said as he rolled his eyes.

KA-CHUNK!

The ground next to the tree city door split open as the trees began to bring up their battle vehicles. The Ortons turned back to look and I could see that they were getting confused about which army they should be concentrating on. The plants were approaching fast as the trees on their battle vehicles were starting to rise into view on their elevator platform. At this rate, both armies would be ready to attack at the exact same moment.

"*Please* let me go!"

I looked over at Karen, who was now struggling to get out of her Orton's grip. With this big of a battle coming, I knew she wouldn't rest until she was a part of it. And yet the Orton was still holding her too tightly for her to do anything except hurt herself if she kept fighting.

The plants suddenly slowed their run and stopped about twenty yards away from us. There was an endless sea of them. And they all looked angry.

Herbert stepped forward and held up his hand.

"Turn around and go back to your city now," he

called as plant language boomed out of his translating disc. "This battle is between my army and the trees. If you enter into it, you too will be destroyed."

The plants all looked at each other as Swiff stepped out from the middle of them.

"We're here to *help* you," she called back to Herbert. "We've been waiting our whole lives to destroy the trees."

"Then both you and the metal army will die today," Gree called out as the elevator holding the battle vehicles locked into place with the entire tree army standing behind them, wearing their armor and holding their weapons. "Because we will not be destroyed. Not now. Not ever."

"Herbert is gonna wipe you out," Swiff yelled back at Gree. "I saw what just a few of the metal guys did to your patrol in the ravine. Look how many there are now. You might as well all just break yourselves in half and save them the trouble."

"Swiff," I called to her, "you've got to help the trees. Herbert's the one who stole your gold and the trees' gold and let you all think you stole it from each other. If you all work together, you might be able to beat his army. But you can't fight on his side. Not after all that he's done to your people."

Swiff's eye narrowed and she glared at me like I was her worst enemy in the world.

"Excuse me, did you say something?" she said sarcastically. "Did I hear some kind of words coming out of your mouth? Because it all just sounded like 'boody biddy blitty butty blatty' to me. So why don't you just stay out of this, you, stupid meat idiot?"

"Swiff, Iggy was mean to you in the ravine to save you," Karen called out. "He was trying to keep you from getting hurt. You've got to do what he's telling you."

"You both must think I'm pretty dumb," she said angrily. "We don't care about the gold. We never did. We just want the trees' city. We're tired of living in a tent. Aren't we, gang?"

The entire plant army let out a loud cheer followed by a long chorus of clicking and rattling. They were definitely all amped up and ready for a fight.

"And just so you know," Swiff said to me coldly, "I never liked you. I only pretended to because I thought you might be able to help us. But now I know you're nothing but a coward. And I can't wait to see you get wiped out in this battle."

Swiff then turned to Herbert. "We know ways to hurt the trees that your army doesn't. We will fight with you if you promise to give us their city once you've destroyed them. Do we have a deal?"

"You have my word," Herbert said with that fakey serious tone of his that I now knew was what he used when he was lying.

"Then let's *do it!*" Swiff yelled as she looked back at the plant army and pointed toward the trees.

"Swiff, please, don't! He'll just kill you too!" I yelled. But it was too late. The plants were clicking and shrieking and making all the noises they made when they were ready for a fight.

Herbert smiled and gave me a smug look that said I had lost, then whistled loudly to the Ortons. They all turned to face the tree army.

The trees started up their battle vehicles with loud roars of the engines.

Blades began to whirl and cables began to spin.

The trees behind them pulled their swords and axes and hatchets off their weapons belts and got ready to charge.

The Ortons all put their right feet forward, as if they were sprinters getting ready for the starting gun at the Olympics.

"Ortons, attack in…*three*…" Herbert yelled as he backed away from the battlefield. "…*tw—*"

"GO!" Swiff yelled early.

I looked over at her, surprised she had cut into Herbert's countdown. The plant army suddenly sprang forward like they had all been shot out of cannons. In an instant, the sky was thick with plants as they flew over my head toward the tree army.

But they didn't attack the tree army.

Instead, they rained down on top of the Ortons like somebody had just dumped a huge bag of lawn clippings on top of a bunch of toy soldiers. Immediately, the plants linked themselves end-to-end, swirled around the metal men, and wrapped them up like mummies. It all happened so fast, the Ortons simply didn't stand a chance.

The metal men struggled to break through all the vines and stems but there were just way too many tied around each of them. In small groups, the plants might not have been strong enough to keep the Ortons from moving their arms and legs, but when thousands of them spun around something, it was like being wrapped up in big thick chains. I knew from the times that Swiff wrapped around me how powerful just one of the plants' stems could be.

Which made me suddenly wonder—where was Swiff?

I looked around but all I could see was an ocean of plants and five hundred tall green vine-wrapped pillars that once were Ortons. I saw the tree army staring in shock, unsure what to think as their battle vehicles idled quietly. And then I saw Herbert standing off to the side, his mouth hanging open with his eyes about to roll out of their sockets from the surprise of it all.

I looked for Karen's Orton but he too was completely wrapped in plants. However, the fingers of his hand had been pulled back and were held open by vines.

Karen was gone.

35
No, She Wasn't

I looked back over at Herbert when suddenly...

CRACK!

From out of nowhere, Karen appeared next to Herbert and punched him right across the face. His eyes rolled back and he fell unconscious onto the ground with a thud.

Karen shook out her hand painfully, then cracked her knuckles. "Man, I was dying to do that," she said with a smile.

FOOM! Something wrapped around me and squeezed me like I was a tube of toothpaste. And the next thing I knew, there was Swiff's huge daisy face about half an inch from my nose.

"We did it, boyfriend! We *did* it!" she yelled, as happy as I'd ever seen her. "Your plan worked!"

"My plan?" I squeaked out with the last bit of air she had left in my crushed lungs.

"You were such a great actor back in the ravine when you were yelling at me and being so mean," she laughed. "I almost believed you for a second. But then I realized that you were telling me to go back to the city, get our army together, pretend like I was mad at you, make Herbert think we were going to help him, and then get his army to turn away from us so we could attack them and wrap them up. You're such a genius! I never could have thought of something like that!"

I looked over at Karen, who had her eyebrow raised at me.

"Gee, Iggy," she said, "it's amazing you communicated all that with just one look. You must really *be* a genius."

"Oh, he is, Karen," Swiff said seriously. "He is."

Oh, man, was this embarrassing.

Realizing that I couldn't take credit for something I didn't do, I was about to tell Swiff the truth when the plants all started cheering in unison, "All hail the Great Meat Master of Games! All hail the Great Meat Master of Games!"

"Get out of the way! Move out of the way!" we heard a voice yell. We looked over and saw Choonk pushing through the plants, followed by Hoosh and Shushle. Choonk shoved his way through and the three of them stopped in front of us.

"Meat Master, are you all right?" Choonk asked, as if he had been really worried about me. "Please tell us you're all right!"

"Yeah, I'm fine," I said, feeling even more embarrassed at all this attention. "We're all fine. You guys did great."

"See, I *told* you he wasn't lying," Swiff said as she poked Hoosh in the stomach.

Just then, we heard a groan. Herbert was starting to wake up from Karen's punch. He put his hand on his jaw and rubbed it, then groggily opened his eyes.

"Hey, guys," Karen said to Choonk and friends. "A little help here."

Swiff pointed at two grape vines who were standing

across from her. They immediately leaped on Herbert and spun around him, tying him up so that he couldn't move.

"This can't be happening again," Herbert said with a shake of his head. He then looked at Karen and me and let out a long sigh. "I give up. You win. I'm finished."

"You certainly are," Hoosh said loudly. "Execute him!"

The plants all cheered as the ones who weren't wrapped around the Ortons started to move toward Herbert, clicking scarily with bloodthirsty looks in their eyes.

"Wait!" I yelled as I put up my hands.

The plants all stopped immediately and stared at me.

"We can't do that," I continued. "First of all, that's the kind of thing he would do. You don't want to be like him, do you? And second, if you kill him, Karen and I will never be able to return your gold because we'll never be able to get back to where he's hidden it. We need him to get to our frequency. But once we're there, I promise you that he'll be punished for all this. We'll make sure of it. Our world is pretty tough on people like him."

"I, too, would like to see him punished right here and now," said Yarg, as he walked through the crowd of plants. "But Iggy is right. The most important thing at this moment is the return of all the gold stolen from us." He then turned to the plants. "And from you."

The plants all stared at Yarg and shifted nervously, clearly uncomfortable being so close to someone they had always considered their enemy. They looked over at the trees, who were still holding their weapons and sitting on their rumbling battle vehicles.

Yarg saw this and turned toward his army. He made a cutting motion with his hand. The soldiers all put their weapons back on their belts and the riders on the vehicles turned off their engines. Yarg then turned to Swiff.

"Thank you for stopping Herbert's army," he said to her. "We owe your people a true debt of gratitude."

He then gave her a friendly look and held out his branch hand to shake her leaf.

We all stood there and waited for Swiff to respond. I couldn't wait to see her smile at him and say you're welcome and then for everything to finally be friendly between the plants and the trees so that Karen and I could leave this frequency in peace and harmony.

"We didn't do it for you," Swiff finally said, in a super snotty way. "We did it for Iggy."

"That's right," Choonk added, stepping forward defiantly, clearly braver than he normally was because he was surrounded by his army. "We did it for the Great Meat Master of Games, military strategist extraordinaire, and genius inventor of soccer, football, baseball, basketball, volleyball, and something called hockey that we still haven't quite figured out yet. When we heard that he wanted Herbert's army destroyed and your city saved, we came here to help *him*. Not any of *you*."

"And if it was up to us," Hoosh said, sticking out his chest and speaking loudly enough for the entire tree army to hear him, "we would have let Herbert's army wipe you out so that we could have taken over your city. So save your thank-yous for someone who believes them."

The plants all started clicking. The Ortons started to shift a bit, as if the plants were loosening their grip. The tree army looked over at Yarg, waiting for his command so they could pull out their weapons and start up their plant-killing machines again.

"You guys, cut it out," I said loudly. "Just be nice to the trees. They're trying to make up with you."

"Do you know how many of us they've mowed down and cut to pieces?" Hoosh said angrily. "They say thank you once and we're supposed to forgive them for all that? Is that how things work in your world?"

"But you were attacking them," Karen said, jumping in. "They had to defend themselves."

"They attacked us, too," Hoosh continued. "They're not innocent in all this."

"They attacked you for the same reason you attacked them," Karen countered. "They thought you had stolen their gold. But neither one of you had. It was all because of this guy right here," she said, pointing at Herbert. "He started this war and turned you against each other just so he could steal what belongs to this frequency. And now we're going to make sure he gets punished for it and get your gold back to you. So stop acting like such babies and make up with the trees."

"But they're bad," Choonk said loudly. "They're mean and evil."

"They lock up their young and force them to do things against their will," Shushle chimed in.

"And they don't let them ever have any fun," Choonk added.

"And they want to do the same thing to us!" Hoosh bellowed. "We know everything about them."

All the plants started yelling and talking over each other as they made angry faces at the trees.

"Wait, quiet down!" I yelled. "None of that's true, is it, Yarg?"

"Actually, it's all true," he announced. "Except for the mean and evil part."

Huh, boy.

"Yarg," I whispered to him, "they're holding five hundred Ortons and one crazy guy who all want to destroy your people. Just say it's not true."

"I will not deny it!" Yarg shouted. "Why should we be ashamed that we raise our young ones to be educated and well behaved? That we don't let them run wild? What do you think our city would we like if we did? I'll tell you what it'd be like. It would be like the plant city."

This started a louder chorus of angry chatter from the plants. The trees pulled their weapons out of their sheaths. The battle vehicles fired up again. The plants arched their backs and started clicking louder than I'd ever heard them click before as the Ortons beneath them started moving, clearly sensing that they were about to be set free.

"WAIT!" I yelled. "DON'T DO THIS!"

"DO IT!" Herbert shouted at the top of his lungs to the plants. "Attack the city with the Ortons and I will give it to you! With my metal army, you cannot be defeated! The trees *did* steal your gold! Iggy and Karen are working with them! They made a deal to subdue you so that you would trust the trees and then enter their city, where they would eliminate you. I know all about it and that's why they want me silenced. You have to believe me! Release the Ortons and attack!"

The plants were now all silent as they stared at Herbert. Hoosh studied him, then turned and looked at me.

"Is what Herbert says true?" he asked me seriously.

"Of course it's not," Karen said.

"I didn't ask you," Hoosh said, not taking his eye off me, like he was trying to see inside my head and read my thoughts. "I asked the Great Meat Master of Games."

"Hoosh, you know it's not true," I said. "We know the whole story. Irk made a deal with Herbert to let him take your gold in exchange for taking Irk back to our frequency. But then Herbert double-crossed him and poisoned Irk, which was why when Irk came back from the ravine the first time he was so sick.

"But Herbert is the one who stole your gold. And if you help him kill the trees, he'll only turn around and kill you, too. Trust me, he tried to kill Karen and me more times than we can count. I know you have problems with the trees and I know that the trees have problems with you. But those problems are nothing compared to the problems you'll have if you do what Herbert Golonski wants you to do."

Hoosh continued to study me as Swiff stepped forward.

"It's true," she said to Hoosh. "We all heard Irk talking to Herbert about it. He helped Herbert steal our gold so that he could go to some place called 'Cally Forny Oar.' Iggy's telling the truth. All Herbert wants is everyone's gold."

Hoosh looked at Herbert, who shook his head and rolled his eyes.

"The daisy is lying," Herbert said with a smug chuckle. "She's in love with Ignatius and will say anything to protect him, even if it means betraying her own people. She's pathetic."

Hoosh nodded slowly, and then bent down and

gently picked Herbert up off the ground, standing him upright on his feet. Herbert smiled, pleased with himself for having gotten through to Hoosh.

Hoosh then leaned in so that his face was inches from Herbert's.

"Are you calling my sister a liar?" he asked quietly.

"Your . . . your sister?" Herbert said nervously.

"Yes," Hoosh said menacingly. "My sister."

And with that, Hoosh picked Herbert up and threw him into the crowd of plants, who all started tossing Herbert over their heads the way a crowd at a baseball game hits a beach ball around in the stands.

"Help!" Herbert yelled as he got bounced off into the distance. "Ouch! Cut it out! Hellllp!"

Hoosh turned back to me and said, "Where is Irk?"

We all looked around and quickly realized we didn't know where he was. Just then, the plants started murmuring about something. I noticed that they were all looking up. I followed their eyes and saw Foo coming down out of the clouds. The plants looked amazed, as did the trees. I had gotten used to seeing Foo flying around but I guess it's pretty crazy the first time you see a really pretty girl all dressed in white, hovering above your head with no strings attached.

"Irk ran back toward the ravine as soon as the attack began," Foo said down to Hoosh. "He looked like he was in quite a hurry."

The plants were so in awe watching Foo flying down that they must have really loosened up their grip on the Ortons, because suddenly several of the metal men broke free.

Hoosh saw this and quickly yelled, "Squeeze them!"

More plants dove back onto the escaping Ortons and tightened around them so hard that we heard the metal men start to bend and crack.

Hoosh then yelled to the plants, "Send the annoying little meat back to us."

Herbert was launched out of the plants on the other side of the battlefield and flew through the air like he was the final pass in the Superbowl.

"YyyyyyyyyyyyyyeeeeeeeeeeeeeeeeeEEEEEEEE-AAAAAAGGGGGGGHHHH!" he yelled as he spiraled toward us.

Hoosh reached up and caught Herbert with one leaf, then plopped him over his shoulder, which made Herbert "OOF!" loudly.

Hoosh then turned to Yarg and said, "Let's go get our gold."

Hey, maybe this wasn't going to be such a bad day
after all.

36
Transporter Bound

Our march back to the ravine must have looked pretty insane from above. The entire tree army *and* the entire plant army escorted us. The plants carried all five hundred Ortons so they could send them back with Herbert. I knew that doing this through the one small transporter in the cave would take forever. But I figured that once we took Herbert back and saw where his headquarters were, there was a good chance I'd discover how he got so many of the Ortons here so quickly in the first place. Then, I'd be able to send them back the same way he got them here: all at once.

When we got to the edge of the ravine, I had the plants stop and wait there. I could imagine the nightmare scenario in which the plants all started hallucinating because of the Good Times gas and suddenly let go of the Ortons. That would be about the worst thing ever, since we were so close to actually getting home and having Herbert thrown in jail.

At first, Hoosh was very suspicious of me wanting to move on without them and thought we were setting the plants up for some kind of ambush or double-cross. But once Swiff and I explained to him how hard it was to get through the ravine without going nuts, he agreed to it. Or at least he did once we said that he and any plant warriors who weren't holding Ortons could come with us.

Since I knew that only the trees seemed to be immune to the Good Times gas, I got them to agree to carry Karen and me and all the plants to the transporter cave so that they could prevent us from running after stuff that wasn't really there. I warned the plants holding the Ortons not to pick up any of the shiny Blevin traps and then the rest of us headed back into the ravine.

The trip to the Cave of Smiles seemed much faster than last time we did it, probably because I now knew exactly where I was going and what to expect along the way. Plus, having experienced the effects of the Good Times gas earlier made it much easier to tell the difference between what was real and what was not. The plants definitely went pretty nutty from the gas, though, and in one especially embarrassing moment, Hoosh started crying because he thought he saw a tiny clover with a small pair of scissors running toward him.

By the time we got to the mouth of the cave, I couldn't stop thinking about how happy I would be to see my parents and how I couldn't wait for Herbert to get his comeuppance. I did worry that the police and the people back home might not believe any of this, but then I realized that if I had a couple of talking trees and plants and a flying girl with me, then someone was going to have to believe I was telling the truth.

As soon as Yarg and the trees saw the cave, they knew that their bodies were just too big to fit inside it. But since no one trusted Herbert and they barely trusted Karen and me to bring their gold back, they recruited a couple of their smallest fighters—two tough little pine trees named Prink and Shangle—to come with us. Hoosh then announced that both he and Swiff would be coming along, too, so that they could keep an eye on the trees and make sure that everything was done fairly. I thought it was really cool that Hoosh now considered his sister responsible enough to be his equal, a respect she had truly earned when she saved the tree city.

And this also made me realize there was something I needed to do.

"You know, everybody," I announced to the plants and trees as we got ready to enter the cave. "Swiff was the one who came up with the plan to stop the Orton army, not me. I just thought you should all know that."

"And…" Karen said, giving me the same look my mom gave me the time she took me over to Ivan's house and made me apologize for putting a rotten banana in his gym shoe so that when he put it on really gross banana jelly squished between his toes and came out the air holes like toothpaste coming out of a tube.

"And…I didn't invent any of those games I told you about," I said, sort of sad to have to give up my title of Great Meat Master of Games. "Soccer and football and all those other sports are actually really popular games from our world that people have been playing forever."

The plants all exchanged a look.

"We don't care who invented them," Choonk said with a shrug. "We're just glad you showed them to us."

"Oh," I said, surprised. "Cool. I just felt like I needed to tell you. We knew a guy in the last world we were in who took credit for things he didn't really invent. I just didn't want to be like him."

Choonk and Shushle nodded but I could tell they had no idea what I was talking about and didn't really care anyway. I think everybody was so preoccupied with the idea of getting their gold back that they just wanted us to go and do it already.

Yarg wished us luck and then gave Hoosh a look that said "Don't try any funny business with our gold." Foo then flew down from the yellow clouds and landed next to me.

I was so happy to see her again that I really felt like hugging her. But it didn't seem like the right place to do it and I also knew that she was so lightweight and fragile that if I did hug her, I might break her in half. And so I took the safe route and smiled at her.

"Thanks for all your help," I said. "I'm really happy to see you again."

"And I'm happy to see you, too," she said, smiling back at me.

Karen rolled her eyes and said, "Okay, Romeo and Juliet, can we just go to the transporter and get these people their gold back?"

Prink and Shangle picked up Herbert, who was still wrapped up by the grape vines, and we started to head into the cave.

"Wait!" Herbert yelled, then looked at Foo. "Do you still have the piece of gold you took from me?"

Foo opened her hand to show that she did.

"Yep, and you're not getting it," Karen said to Herbert, clearly enjoying having him powerless in front of her.

"I don't want it," he snapped back at her. Then he caught himself and tried to sound nice. "I just wanted to make sure that we didn't take it with us. I want to give it back to the people of this frequency."

"Gee, do you really?" Karen said sarcastically. "Wow, you're such a great guy. Any other nice generous things you want to do, like let them keep their leaves or allow them to continue breathing?"

Herbert stared at Karen for a few seconds, then forced an insincere smile at her.

"I just wanted to make sure we didn't take it with us," he said again. "That's all."

Foo held out the gold to Yarg. However, just as he was reaching for it, Hoosh stepped forward and put his hands on his hips.

"Wait a minute," Hoosh said suspiciously. "Why do *they* get to keep it?"

"Because there's only one piece," Karen answered as if Hoosh's question was really stupid.

"But why does it go to them and not to us?" Choonk said, stepping forward and staring at the gold in Foo's hand.

"You guys, seriously," Karen said impatiently. "Are you really going to start a fight over this? You're as bad as Herbert."

"This is the kind of immaturity we have grown to expect from the One Ringers," Yarg said as he looked at Gree and the trees around him, who nodded in agreement.

"Who you calling 'immature?'" Hoosh said like he was getting ready for a fight.

"You guys, *please*," I said, "don't do this. Just let Yarg

hold the gold for now. Pretty soon you'll have tons of it and you can divide it up fairly."

"We're not going anywhere until we get half of that gold," Hoosh said as he crossed his leaves and stood his ground.

"This is why our cities will never have peace," Yarg said loudly. "The One Ringers will never learn. They don't grow old enough to mature. They can't be taught and they can't behave responsibly. We will never have any—"

"Yarg, shut up!" I yelled.

"Yeah!" Hoosh laughed. "You tell him, Iggy!"

"You shut up too!" I snapped at Hoosh. "All of you, just shut up for once. You guys have to work this all out. It's ridiculous."

The whole crowd of plants and trees just stood and stared at me, surprised. But I was really fed up with all of them and couldn't believe that things were about to fall apart right when we were so close to solving all their problems.

"Hoosh, you and your people need to stop acting like such idiots."

"Hey!" Choonk said, insulted.

"I'm sorry but it's true," I said. "Can't you all see

how silly you look to the trees? You act exactly the way they think you're going to act—like a bunch of babies. Do you think it's cool or something to be so wild and out of control all the time? Don't you see that's why the trees can't stand you? Why they can't trust you?"

"Finally, somebody speaks the truth!" Yarg said with a laugh.

"Hey, you guys are just as bad," I said, spinning to face Yarg. "You're obsessed with all your rules and with trying to control everything and passing judgment on everybody. Did you ever try to teach anybody anything without locking them up in rooms for years and not letting them have any fun at all? Your city seems totally boring because you guys are so afraid of people having fun. Maybe if you all had a good time once in a while you wouldn't always be so angry."

"You have no idea what you're talking about," Yarg said as he glared at me.

"Maybe I don't but whatever you guys are doing it isn't working," I said back. "This frequency is totally messed up. And I don't even want to bring your gold back if it means that nothing's going to change. Why don't you guys let the plants into your city once in a while? Let them get some of your sunlight so they don't have to drink dark all the time. Talk to them and tell them all the things you've learned over the years since you're so much older than they are.

"I bet that if you guys were nice to them and showed them what cool Multi-Ringers act like they'd stop hating you so much. Otherwise, you're all just going to end up destroying each other, gold or no gold."

Yarg stared at me, then leaned forward like he was going to say something. But he didn't. I could tell he didn't know what to say. I looked over at the plants, who were staring at me pretty much the same way that Yarg was. *Nobody* knew what to say.

Finally, Yarg reached out and gently took the gold piece from Foo as Hoosh and the plants watched him cautiously. He then bent the little gold brick in the middle and worked it back and forth until it broke in half.

Yarg held out one of the halves to Hoosh. Hoosh looked at Yarg like he wasn't sure what to do, then slowly reached out and took the half piece of gold. Choonk stretched his neck and looked at the gold in Hoosh's hand.

"I think Yarg's piece is a little bigger," Choonk said quietly.

Hoosh smacked Choonk in the back of the head and then nodded at Yarg.

"Thanks," Hoosh said. He flipped the half piece of gold to Shushle for safekeeping and then turned to me. "Let's go."

And with that, we all headed into the cave that would take us back home.

37
Going Home

If someone had a camera, we would have made a pretty weird picture.

Two pine trees, two big flowers, two kids, one flying girl, and one bad guy tied up by living grape vines, all standing under a transporter gate waiting to jump frequencies. And yet, standing there in the middle of it all, it seemed totally normal to me.

Which showed me just exactly how bizarre my life had gotten since I became a Frequenaut.

At first, it seemed like we might never get to jump frequencies because Herbert refused to program the transporter. The pine trees and Karen threatened Herbert and Hoosh even tried to force him to put his hands on the computer screen. But it's pretty hard to force someone to do something they don't want to do, especially when you have no idea how to do it yourself. All the info on how to make a transporter jump frequencies was inside Herbert's head and so if he didn't want to help, then there was very little we could do about it.

But then Foo told Herbert how important it was that he do the right thing and get everyone their gold back and return us to the frequencies that we missed. She was so sweet and sincere that it seemed like she actually melted Herbert's heart. Which was surprising to all of us because we assumed he didn't have one.

He smiled at her, said, "Okay," and then he waved his fingers over the computer screen. Then the lights on the transporter gate came on and the machine started to hum. Hoosh then picked up Herbert and put him under the gate with us since the grape vines were still wrapped around him so that he couldn't run away.

"You had better be taking us to the right frequency,"

Karen said threateningly to Herbert. "Because if you don't, we will not be kind to you."

"I guarantee that you are about to see more gold than you have ever seen in your life," he said with a sincere smile. "Trust me."

"That's not the answer I was looking for," Karen said as the machine began to hum louder and louder. She then said to Hoosh, "Stay close to him."

As Hoosh flexed his flower muscles and gave Herbert the evil eye, the machine glowed brighter and I began to feel the weightlessness in my chest you get right before you jump frequencies. I looked over at Karen, who gave me a look back that said she was worried.

I forced a smile at her and said, "We're going home."

"I hope so," she said back as the humming got to a deafening level. "I really hope so."

Prink and Shangle were looking around nervously as Swiff was holding the sides of her head, trying to block out the sound. Hoosh was trying to look like he wasn't scared but his eye was pretty wide with fear. I then felt something light and soft take my hand and when I looked down, Foo's fingers were wrapped around mine. I gave her a smile and she smiled back at me and

I realized that I was actually going to have a beautiful flying girlfriend back in my own frequency for a little while. It almost seemed too good to be true.

Which is usually the feeling you have right before everything goes horribly wrong.

Right as the humming hit its loudest level and the lights were so bright that none of us could see, Herbert yelled, "NOW!"

WHAM!

From out of nowhere, Irk flew out of the bright

cloud of light and hit Hoosh, Swiff, and the trees hard from behind with his trunk. Swiff screamed as they all flew forward out of the transporter like they had been smacked by a huge baseball bat. As Swiff was launched, I guess she must have reached out to try and grab onto something to keep her from falling because the next thing I knew, I felt Foo's hand get yanked out of mine. I saw her face look back at me helplessly as she went flying with Swiff's leaf holding onto her arm.

"Iggy!" she yelled as I saw her disappear into the cloud of light surrounding us.

And then...

BOOM!!!

The light exploded and the ground shook and I felt the air around my body burst inward as Karen and I fell against each other and onto the ground.

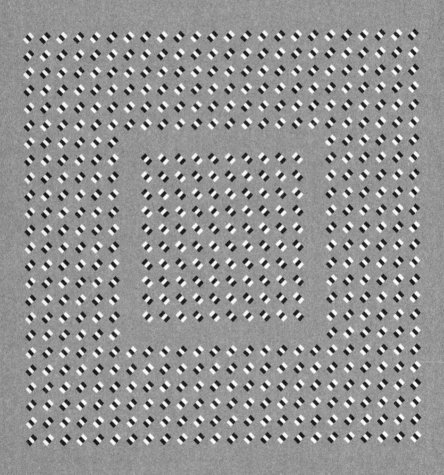

38
Hyglen

All the noise stopped. Everything went silent.

And suddenly I felt like my head exploded.

But not in a painful way. It was more like somebody removed the top of my skull and then blew up my brain like a huge balloon. But it happened so fast that I immediately got dizzy and disoriented.

Light flooded into my eyes so brightly that I had to close them. But closing them didn't seem to stop the light from coming in. It was like there was a big glowing lamp inside my huge expanding brain.

I heard Karen say "Oh, man" in a shaky voice and then fall against me.

I squinted to see her but I couldn't get my eyes to adjust. Everything was too bright. I could only make out a fuzzy image of her holding her head.

"Karen, do you feel weird?" I asked.

"I feel like I'm gonna throw up," she said, sounding as dizzy as I was feeling. "Where are we?"

"I don't know," I said back, still trying to squint through the light. "I can't see anything."

"Welcome to Hyglen," we heard Herbert say. "You are officially in the highest frequency there is. Feels wonderful, doesn't it?"

I forced my eyes to focus through the brightness and saw Herbert standing about ten feet in front of us. He had a big happy smile on his face and was slowly taking the grape vines off him. They had gone completely limp and I could tell by their eyes that whatever it was that was making Karen and me feel so weird had completely fried their tiny brains. As Herbert dropped them onto the ground like wet ropes, my eyes adjusted enough to let me see where we were...

In the middle of an endless white room filled with stacks of gold bars piled ten stories high. It was like sitting in the center of a city made entirely of gold bricks. The building this room was in must have been enormous because I couldn't even see the ceiling. It was just infinite white over the massive stacks of gold.

When I looked back over at Herbert, I saw Irk lying on the ground next to him. He was sprawled out facedown and I couldn't tell if he was alive or dead. Herbert gave him a nudge with his foot and Irk suddenly jumped up and hit his fighting stance like he thought he was about to be attacked.

"Did I do it?" he yelled out. "Did I get rid of all the guards in time? Did I knock them out of the transporter?"

"You did wonderfully, my friend," Herbert said to him.

Irk's eye then went wide as whatever thing Karen's and my brain had experienced must have hit his brain, too. He swooned back and forth a couple of times and then fell over.

"What's happening?" Irk said as he grabbed his head. "Why do I feel like this?"

"You're all going to feel a little odd until you get used to it," Herbert said, sounding a way I'd never heard him sound before—really happy. I mean, he was practically laughing as he spoke, like he was some girl in love or something. "But once you get used to it, you'll never want the feeling to go away."

"What did you do to the air in here?" Karen said as she tried to focus her eyes but couldn't.

"It has nothing to do with the air. You are merely experiencing a wider bandwidth than your brains have ever experienced before. This is the highest and widest frequency that exists and because of it, the Hyglenians are not trapped in a three-dimensional world. Their world is expanded. And even though we are trapped in our bodies from that ghastly frequency in which we were born, our brains respond and expand in the freedom of an enlarged reality. And what you're feeling right now is what it's like to use your entire brain."

"What are you talking about?" Karen said impatiently as she held her head like she was trying to keep it from breaking apart. "And stop talking so loud."

"Do you know how much of your brain you use back in our frequency?" Herbert asked, getting more excited by the second. "Ten percent. *Ten percent!* The smartest people who ever lived in our world only used *ten percent* of their brains. Einstein, da Vinci. Ninety percent of their brains sat in their heads unused. But here...here we have access to *one hundred percent* of our brains! And do you know what that means? Do you know what we can do if we learn to use that power?"

And before we could answer, Herbert pointed his finger at Karen and me and we slowly began to lift off the ground. He pointed higher and higher and we floated up higher and higher and I thought that I either had to be dreaming or that we were dead and this was some sort of weird version of the afterlife.

But it was neither.

It was real.

And it was freaking me out majorly.

"Put us down!" Karen yelled. "Take us back to our frequency! Why did you bring us here anyway?"

"Because I've decided that I need you," Herbert said casually. "I had always planned on simply eliminating the two of you. But in the last two frequencies, you proved yourselves to be quite resourceful. I could use a couple of smart young people like yourselves on my team."

"You have *got* to be joking." Karen laughed. "You absolutely *cannot* be serious. After all you've done to us and to the people we've met? After all the destruction and problems you've caused? You think we would *ever* do *anything* to help you keep stealing gold? Now, *that* is hilarious."

"Oh, it's not that funny," he said with a smile. "And you *will* do whatever I tell you. That I can guarantee."

Herbert pointed to the left and we began to float over to what looked like a big laboratory area. There were lots of strange machines that looked like they had been built by the same people who made the transporter gates. As we floated down toward all this, I saw there were several futuristic-looking dentist-type chairs in front of a row of tall thin machines. One of the chairs had some sort of cloudy bright bubble of light surrounding it and as we got closer, I could see that there was a person inside. I squinted to look closer and realized something.

It was Chester Arthur!

You know, the former English teacher who was a dictator in the last frequency we were in and who followed Herbert to this frequency by jumping into the transporter at the last second—with my dad's super expensive Shakespeare book?

Well, it was him.

"Karen," I said, weirded out. "It's Mr. Arthur."

He looked like he was in a trance. His eyes were open but they weren't looking at anything. And there was a low humming sound coming from two small computer screens on either side of his head that were flashing patterns of light onto his temples.

We started to descend and saw we were being lowered onto two of the empty chairs next to him.

"Oh, forget this!" Karen said as she tried to move out of the way.

But both she and I quickly realized we couldn't do anything. Not only were we floating but Herbert was somehow controlling all our limbs. It felt like we had a bunch of hands holding our arms and legs in place and they were now pulling us into a sitting position so that we would fit perfectly in the bubble chairs.

"Let us go, Herbert!" Karen yelled. "I don't know what you're doing to Chester but you are *not* doing it to us!"

"Don't worry," Herbert said as he lowered us into the chairs. "This is a good thing. I am doing something wonderful for you. Something you will both thank me for. In fact, what I'm doing for you is almost too nice considering the way you two have treated me since we met. But, hey, let's let bygones be bygones, shall we?"

"What, are you gonna reprogram our brains or something, you psycho?" she snapped. "So we'll be happy to do whatever you want us to do? Is that the plan?"

"In a nutshell, yes," Herbert said with a shrug. "But you will also know everything about this frequency. You'll know how to use all the powers that come from living in a world with extra dimensions and having that glorious extra ninety percent of your brain working on all cylinders. The only difference will be that you'll actually enjoy it all and will see that what I'm doing in all these frequencies is the right thing. It's pretty much a win-win situation for you, if you ask me."

Our bodies pressed down onto the chairs as if we were being strapped into them by invisible seat belts.

"You're really insane, do you know that?" Karen hissed. "How can stealing more gold than you can ever use be the right thing to do?"

"You think this is only about *gold*?" Herbert laughed. "You really have a low opinion of me, don't you? This is about the future. But you're going to learn about all that right now."

He pointed at the machines behind our chairs. They both lit up and began to quietly hum like the one behind Mr. Arthur. Our heads were pushed down onto the headrests as colors began flashing and darting through the air and then a bubble of light formed around each of us. I fought to keep my mind from drifting away but it suddenly felt like I was really tired and that I was having a flying dream and all I wanted to do was fall asleep and enjoy it.

Which I knew wouldn't be a good thing. Not if it meant being Herbert Golonski's slave once I woke up.

No way.

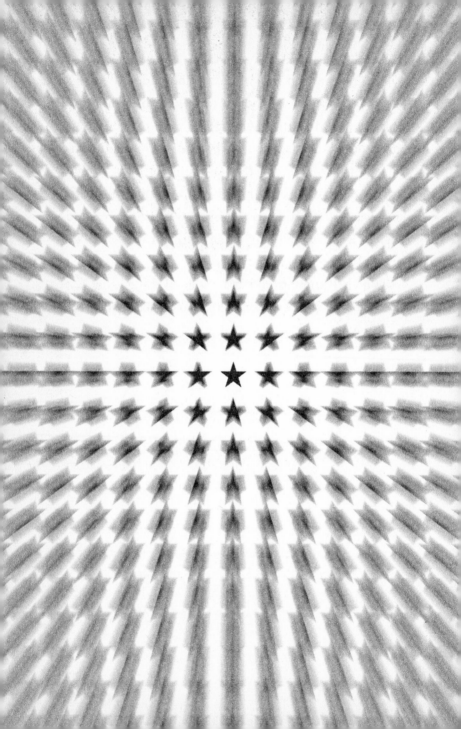

39
Do or Die

"Karen," I said as I tried to keep focused. "You're stronger than Herbert. You know you can overpower him in any fight. Take him down. You're the only one who can."

Karen stared at me and I could see she was having a hard time staying awake, too. But then she looked at her trapped body and her face turned angry. She nodded at me and then began to tense up her muscles like she was trying to fight against whatever was holding her onto the chair.

Herbert looked surprised. He stepped forward and saw that Karen's hand was starting to shake as she began to lift it off the chair. He quickly pointed at her and her hand slammed back down. But then she took a breath and her face got red as she began to strain even harder to lift her arm.

Slowly, her hand began to rise off the chair again. Herbert pointed at her more intensely and now *his* face was starting to get red as he strained to keep her down using his brain power. Karen was shaking as her face practically turned purple and I began to worry that her head was going to explode.

"Do…not…do…this," Herbert struggled to say as every muscle in his body was tensed in battle against Karen. "If you do not cooperate, I will have you destroyed. I don't need you that badly."

"You're gonna destroy me?" Karen said as she began to sit up, her whole body shaking with force. "You and what *army*?"

And with that she thrust herself forward and jumped up off the chair. The force of this sent Herbert flying backward. He crashed onto the ground, then sat up quickly.

"No!" he yelled. "You are *not* winning this time!"

He pointed hard as she ran at him, stopping her in her tracks like she had been hit in the face. Karen stumbled backward, then took a breath and concentrated. She thrust her hand at Herbert, making him slide back a few more feet. He pointed at her and she stumbled again. She did the same back at him and it started to look like they were having a big arm wrestling match with their minds.

"Irk!" Herbert yelled as he battled with Karen. "You want to go to California? Then take care of her once and for all."

Irk looked over but we could all see that in the condition he was in, he posed no threat to Karen or to anyone else for that matter. He just stood there with his fronds drooping down and his trunk hunched over like an old man.

"Okay," he said weakly. "Just give me a minute to get my bearings."

"If that's your backup," Karen said as she strained to keep Herbert at bay, "then you are in serious trouble."

"Let's just say that my backup simply needs a little nourishment," Herbert said with an evil smile.

Herbert then pointed up at the high white ceiling with the hand he wasn't using to fight Karen and made a swirling motion. The ceiling began to spin like it was a hurricane cloud and a big hole opened up in the center. Bright blue sky appeared as sunlight flooded in and down onto all of us.

As the sun hit Irk, he looked up at the sky, smiled, and then held out his fronds. His entire body was now completely covered in sunlight.

His posture began to straighten as the color flooded back into his trunk and fronds. His whole body started to look stronger as he quickly transformed back into the palm tree we had first met in the tree city jail. It was like when Popeye ate a can of spinach in those old cartoons.

"I...feel...GREAT!!!" he shouted to the sky as he held up his arms, then spun and threw a kung fu kick and a double punch at the air. "Is this what it feels like in California?"

"It's even better there," Herbert called over with one of his big fake smiles.

"Then, Karen," Irk said as he looked over at her and gave her an apologetic shrug, "I'm afraid I have to take care of you. Once and for all."

"Yeah?" she said as she squinted at him through angry eyes. "Let's see you try."

Karen then thrust both her hands toward Herbert.

He flew off his feet and slammed into one of the big transporters, which fell over and boomed heavily onto the floor. Herbert landed on top of it hard and let out a big holler of pain as he grabbed his back. Karen then spun and hit her kung fu stance as she faced off with Irk.

"Game on, tree boy," she said with a smile, then launched into a vicious attack.

Karen and Irk were a flurry of punches and kicks and spins as they both fought with more power and energy than they ever had before. They were both feeling good, and in the few moments that I could actually see Karen's face as she moved and jumped in a blur of motion, it looked to me like she had a big smile.

As their fight continued, I saw that Herbert was still lying on top of the fallen transporter, moaning in pain. I tried to use the moment to get up but I still felt the invisible belts holding me down. I guess once Herbert put them on you, they stayed there whether he was paying attention or not. But now that I'd seen Karen use her strength to get out of the invisible belts he put around her, I figured that maybe I could do the same now that Herbert was in such bad shape.

I strained and tightened all my muscles as hard as I could, just like Karen did. But all that resulted from this method was an immediate headache and the cutting of a huge fart.

"Gross!" I heard Karen yell as she did a big spinning sweep kick that Irk barely avoided. "Control yourself, Iggy."

As embarrassed as I was, Karen's words made me realize something. If what Herbert was saying about having all this extra brain power was true, then there must be some way to control things the way that Herbert did without having to be super strong. I mean, Herbert was in terrible shape and pretty old but he could still make us float and put invisible belts around us with his mind.

And so I took a deep breath, tried to relax, and thought to myself, "Remove the belts that are holding me down."

I tried to lift my hand.

Nothing was stopping it.

I sat up.

No belts were holding me.

Man, I thought, having all this extra brain power is really cool.

Just then, Herbert sat up. He saw that Karen had her back to him as she fought with Irk. Seeing his chance to do her in for good, Herbert pointed over at a huge heavy transporter and lifted it into the air. He then whipped his hand toward Karen, sending the giant transporter flying directly at her.

"NO!" I yelled as I thrust my hand at the speeding piece of machinery while I thought, "Push that away from Karen!"

Karen turned just in time to see the metal thing about to crush her. But at the last second, my command made the huge transporter veer to the left and shoot past her, missing her by less than an inch.

And then…

CRASH!

The transporter smashed right into the bottom of one of the huge ten-story-high stacks of gold bricks. It hit it so hard that it pushed a ton of bricks out the other side of the pile and made a huge hole in the base.

Everything went quiet.

Then there was a rumble as we saw the bricks start to fall one by one into the hole.

"Oh no," Herbert said as he jumped to his feet.

Clink. Clink. Clink.

The bricks kept falling, more and more at a time. And then…

ROAR!

The whole sky-high stack of gold caved in like one

of those old hotels or office buildings they blow up on TV when they want to tear it down.

Herbert threw up his hands to try and stop it from falling, but it was too late.

"RUN!" Karen yelled, grabbing my hand and yank-

ing me off the chair as we sprinted away from the tidal wave of bricks.

I looked back as we ran and saw Mr. Arthur lying inside his bubble chair. I just couldn't let him get crushed under a mountain of gold.

I reached my hand back and thought, "Bring Mr. Arthur with us."

His chair started to roll after us like a race car. As it moved away from the machine it was in front of, the bubble surrounding it disappeared. And suddenly, Mr. Arthur sat up like he had just woken up from a nightmare.

"What's going on?" he yelled. Then he saw Karen and me running ahead of him. "Iggy? Karen? Is that you?"

"We'll catch up on old times later," Karen called over her shoulder as Mr. Arthur looked back and saw the avalanche of gold bricks falling after us. As they surged forward, they smashed into the other ten-story-high stacks of gold bars, which also started to collapse.

We looked ahead and saw that we were running toward a dead end. The stacks of gold bricks on either side of us created an alley that ended at the white wall of the warehouse. We were trapped and there was no way we weren't going to be completely crushed by the tidal wave of gold bricks chasing after us.

I saw the transporter gates up ahead and knew that our only hope was to get out of this frequency at that very moment.

"Over there!" I yelled as I pointed at the transporters. "We're getting out of this place."

"But we don't know how to use them!" Karen yelled.

"You got a better plan?" I said as I yanked her toward them.

We looked back over our shoulder and saw Herbert standing in the open area behind us, about to get crushed under the wave of gold bricks. But he wasn't running. He was just standing there.

"Oh, well," he called after us, shrugging his shoulders. "I tried."

He then pointed at his feet and suddenly the floor swirled open beneath him.

"Nice knowing you," he said with a smile, then dropped through the hole, which spun shut just as the wall of gold bricks swept over it.

BLAM!

The gold hit the huge stack next to us, which pushed the bottom bricks inward and made the whole pile begin to tip forward. We had a few seconds to get that transporter to work or we were going to be buried under the most expensive avalanche ever.

I ran up to the computer screen on a small transporter and waved my fingers over the screen the way I had seen Herbert do.

Of course, nothing happened.

"We're so dead," Karen said as she watched the massive wall of gold bricks falling toward us.

"Wait!" Mr. Arthur said as he jumped off the rolling chair and ran up to the screen. "I don't know why but I think I know what to do."

"You were in the reprogramming machine!" I yelled. "You must have some of the information about how to work it in your brain. Try to start it!"

Mr. Arthur looked at the screen, his eyes filling with panic.

"I can't think!" he yelled. "My head's all scrambled up."

"Don't think!" I yelled at him. "Just clear your brain and ask yourself one thing. 'How do I jump frequencies?'"

He closed his eyes and took a deep breath.

"Iggy, it's over," Karen said as the bricks started to rain down around us.

"No way!" I yelled. "I'm not dying here!"

"I GOT IT!" Chester yelled. "I KNOW WHAT TO DO!"

He danced his fingers across the computer screen and suddenly the transporter lit up like a Christmas tree.

"GET IN!" I yelled as I grabbed Karen's arm.

The three of us crammed inside. The transporter's hum grew quickly as we all looked up and saw millions of bricks about to crash down on top of us.

"If we don't make it, Chester," Karen said, "thanks for trying."

And just as the bricks hit the top of the transporter...

40
BOOM!!!

We woke up on what felt like a sheet of glass.

The three of us were lying in a heap under the transporter, which was now sitting silently. I looked around and saw that we were in another frequency, but it clearly wasn't home.

Huge jagged shafts of white crystals were sticking up at a million different angles, like twenty-foot-high sticks of rock candy that somebody had stuck into the ground. They went on in all directions as far as we could see. In the distance, giant ten-story-high amoeba-like blob creatures were walking slowly through the crystal shafts, some of them bent over and sucking on the tops of taller pink-colored crystals like they were popsicles. None of them seemed to notice us or care that we were there. They were simply going about their business.

"Nice work getting us out of there, Chester," Karen said as she propped herself up on her arms and gave him an appreciative smile. "Now, could you get your foot out of my back?"

"Where are we?" he asked as he shifted his leg.

"Don't you know?" I asked. "You're the one who set the machine."

"I only knew how to make it jump frequencies," he said, looking up at the transporter. "There are like thousands of codes in my head that I know are frequencies, but I don't know anything more specific than that. I guess the rest of the information about them hadn't been downloaded into my brain yet when you took me off the machine."

"So, you know how to work the transporter but you have no idea where it's gonna take us?" Karen asked with her eyebrow raised.

"Um…" Mr. Arthur said, looking embarrassed. "Yep. That's pretty much it."

"O-kay." Karen sighed.

The three of us stood up and looked out at the strange landscape of this new frequency. And even though I knew we had to find Foo, get everyone their gold, and then get ourselves back home, I was actually feeling pretty good about things.

"Well, at least we have our own transporter," I said as I watched a giant amoeba stand up from the crystal it was sucking on and stare over at us with a curious look. "And if we made it out of the last two frequencies alive, I have a pretty good feeling that we can figure out how to make this thing take us where we want to go. Um…eventually."

"Yeah, and that would be great because we have to stop Herbert," Mr. Arthur said. "You probably don't know this but he's getting ready to use his gold to destroy all the frequencies. Well, except the one he lives in now."

"How's he going to destroy them?" Karen asked as we both stared at him in shock. "And *why?*"

"I have no idea," Mr. Arthur said. "But, trust me, he's going to do it. And soon."

Karen and I exchanged a look.

"Not if we stop him first," Karen said.

"You really think we can?" Mr. Arthur asked.

"I don't see why not," I said as I gave Karen a smile. "So, why don't you type one of those frequencies into the computer and let's see where this thing takes us. Because there's no way we can stop him if we stay here."

Mr. Arthur set the machine to one of the unknown frequencies in his head and we all got inside the transporter. As it started to glow and hum, I realized just how much work we had ahead of us.

But I didn't mind.

I was ready for anything.

You have to be if you're a Frequenaut, you know.